★★★★★ *"I have always loved Susan Hatler's romances... but this one goes to another level."*
— Marsha @ Keeper Bookshelf on *The Christmas Compromise*

★★★★★ *"Ms. Hatler has a way of writing witty dialogue that makes you laugh out loud throughout her stories."*
— Night Owl Reviews

★★★★★ *"I couldn't help but smile and laugh at the antics that Ben and Sarah go through. I'm so excited for this whole series!"*
— Katie's Clean Book Collection re *The Wedding Charm*

★★★★★ *"The Friendliest Festival is a wonderful and perfect release to a stressful or crazy day."*
— Cafè of Dreams Book Reviews

★★★★★ *"Susan Hatler's books always give me butterflies and swoony feelings with flirty banter and fun characters."*
— Getting Your Read On Reviews

★★★★★ *"Susan Hatler is the best at clean romcom and this one is at the top of my favorite list."*
— YeahOrNeighReviews on *Million Dollar Date*

TITLES BY SUSAN HATLER

TITLES BY SUSAN HATLER

Do-Over Date Series
Million Dollar Date
The Double Date Disaster
The Date Next Door
Date to the Rescue
The Dashing Date
Once Upon a Date
The Island Date
One Fine Date
The Date Mistake
The Decadent Date

The Wedding Whisperer Series
The Wedding Charm
The Wedding Connection
My Wedding Date
The Wedding Bet
The Wedding Promise

TITLES BY SUSAN HATLER

Montana Dreams Series

The Friendliest Festival

The Delightful Dinner

The Brightest Boutique

The Memorable Mountain

The Welcoming Wedding

The Happiest Hike

The Sweetest Surprise

The Comforting Christmas

Young Adult Novels

See Me

The Crush Dilemma

Shaken

THE HAPPIEST PLACE

SUSAN HATLER

The Happiest Place
(previously published as Love at First Date)
Copyright © 2012 by Susan Hatler

All rights reserved. Without limiting the rights under copyright reserved above, no part of this publication may be reproduced, stored in or introduced into a retrieval system, or transmitted, in any form, or by any means (electronic, mechanical, photocopying, recording, or otherwise) without the prior written permission of the copyright owner of this book. This is a work of fiction. Names, characters, places, brands, media, and incidents are either the product of the author's imagination or are used fictiously.

ISBN: 9798296614704

Cover Design by Elaina Lee, For The Muse Design

💜 **Join Susan's inner circle** for sneak peeks, swoon-worthy updates, and first dibs on her fresh, flirty & fabulous new releases—**subscribe now at** susanhatler.com/newsletter

THE HAPPIEST PLACE

SUSAN HATLER

CHAPTER ONE

WHEN IT COMES TO MEN, I'm a practical girl. Well, woman. I just celebrated my thirtieth birthday last month. Anyway, stars and fireworks where guys are concerned? Love deep enough to be my happy place? Total fantasy. I blame the movies for all that hype.

After two failed marriages, my mom learned with Hubby Number Three that lasting relationships are all about compatibility, which is why I recently signed up at Detailed Dating—a popular Sacramento online dating site. I'm going to save precious time (not to mention frustration and heartache) learning the 411 about a potential mate up front to see if we'll make it for the long haul. Museums and musicals? Yes. Computer games and fantasy football? No, thanks.

After six weeks of email exchanges, I've narrowed it down to two prospects: *lookn4luv* and *jusUnME*. Both guys appear to have interests and goals compatible with mine, and our email exchanges have gone well, so I'm stoked about taking the next step in the Detailed Dating process by scheduling "face-to-face" coffee dates (separately, of course).

As I typed a customer complaint report on my computer at work, I was pondering which potential mate to date first when my best friend's face popped over the cubicle partition between us.

"Ellen?" Rachel's head tilted to the side and her brown hair fell against her cheek. "You got a sec?"

"Sure." As she made her way over to me, I pushed my upcoming dates out of my mind, finished addressing Gilbert Watson's claim that our software program had made his laptop go wonky (I used more professional terms, of course), then swiveled in my office chair to face her. "What's up? You can't complain about work yet. It's only Monday afternoon."

"Very funny." She strode to my desk, picked up my Detailed Dating pen—which was emblazoned with hearts—and started clicking it open and closed obsessively.

I eyed her closely. "Something wrong?"

"No." Her voice strained too emphatically for me to buy. "Everything's great. I mean, Chester's had a hard time adjusting to the move and all, but he's doing better for sure."

She had recently moved into her own apartment in lieu of the rental house she'd been sharing with roommates. But, hello? What difference should that make to her pooch? "Honestly, Rach. You worry too much about Chester's mental stability. He's a dog. As long as he has food and water, he's fine. Stop worrying."

"Pfft." She gave an exaggerated shrug. "Who's worried?"

My eyes narrowed suspiciously. Something was definitely up. Rachel had adopted her miniature beagle a few months ago and treated him like a king. Although she'd wanted her own place for eons, she now felt selfish for uprooting him from the home he'd known and loved.

Spare me.

"Whatever's going on, dish." I gestured toward the overloaded in-box on my desk. "I've got a stack of customer complaints the VPs want me to get through before lunch."

"Well, since you brought up Chester . . ." She used a tone that suggested she'd suddenly thought of something. "Perhaps you'd like to come over tonight and bond with him. He'd love a little one-on-one auntie time since he feels so bad about Saturday."

I glanced down at the gorgeous pair of heeled boots on my feet. I'd only worn them once before her mutt had gnawed on them like his own personal rawhide. "Honestly, Rachel, are you trying to hurt me? You know how expensive these were."

"Ellen, you have to forgive him. I mean, how's my sweet puppy supposed to know the difference between a pair of shoes and a chew toy?" She eyed the savage marks in my leather boots and grimaced. "I'll buy you a new pair when we get paid Friday."

"No, no . . ." Rach and I were both on a tight budget, which is why I'd turned down the sleek and sexy red stilettos I'd drooled over and instead bought the practical black boots I'd use more often. Even with Chester's teeth marks. "I mean, they're not completely ruined, just damaged. Train him to stay away from my footwear and we'll call it good."

"Working on it." Her eyes darted left then right as if someone might be eavesdropping. "But, in the meantime. . . I need a favor."

Rachel Price had been my best friend for over four years, and there wasn't anything I wouldn't do for her. "Sure." I lowered my voice. "What is it?"

She bit her lip. "I need you to come over and baby-sit Chester tonight."

I leaned forward, burst out laughing, and waited for her to join in. When she didn't, my face froze mid-giggle. "You're serious?"

"Ellen." She put a hand on my arm. "It's an emergency."

"Hmm. How can I put this in a way you'll understand?" I tapped an index finger against my temple. "Illness, bleeding, dying . . . *emergencies*. Puppy-sitting? Not so much."

Rachel groaned. "I wouldn't ask unless it was urgent."

My brows rose. "I'll bite. What's the 911?"

"You know Gina in accounting?"

"Of course." Gina interrupts me several times each week with a bookkeeping *emergency*. I use that term loosely. It's all a ruse so she can come into my cubicle to angst over when George will propose. Not like I'd hold my breath on that one. They'd been living together for a decade now.

"Well, Gina wants to set me up with George's friend.

4

They have four tickets to see that new 80s band at The Oasis tonight." She took a deep breath. "I'd really like to go."

"You would?" I gasped. This news was huge. Rachel had spent the last six months mourning her two-year relationship with Jeremy — a guy who'd had the nerve to hook up with her hairdresser behind her back several weeks before dumping her. She'd been heartbroken and unwilling to trust guys since (can't blame her there). If she wanted to get back in the game, that must mean she's finally over the douche bag. Yay!

Unfortunately, I had my own plans this evening. Me, my laptop, and *lookn4luv* versus *jusUnME*. "Can't Chester hang by himself at your apartment while you go on your double date? After all, he's home alone right now."

Her face scrunched up. "He's still adjusting to the move, and he's expecting me to be home after work. He'll be sad and lonely if I desert him during his emotional crisis. I can't dismiss his feelings because a hot guy shows up."

I sat up a little straighter. The plot thickened. "He's hot, huh?"

"Like you wouldn't believe." She reached inside her handbag and pulled out a small photo. "Gina said it's from a year ago, but still."

I gazed appreciatively at the dazzling display of manhood in the beach photo. Golden hair slicked back from the surf, a smile that showed off his pearly whites, and drops of water that glistened on a tanned, muscular chest. "Wowzers."

Her face lit up. "I know, right?"

"Hmm." Even so, without a detailed profile, I'd be reluctant to go on a date even with this hottie. There's no telling what kind of whacky habits the guy had or whether they shared anything in common. My mom's second husband had been handsome, but after two years leading separate lives due to different interests, they'd called it quits.

"So?" She gave me a desperate look, then sighed. "Come on. You're my best friend and the only one I trust to take care of my baby."

I scoffed. "Correction, your dog."

She tapped the cheerful red pen against her palm. "I didn't want to bring this up ever, believe me, but remember when you made me watch that awful movie last year? Do you have any idea how long I was traumatized by that depressing boxer film? When that girl begged her trainer to end her life?"

"That was not my fault." I pointed a finger at her. "My mom recommended it and said we'd love it." Not.

"Nightmares, Ellen. For months." Rachel's eyes grew serious. "Come on. I won't have a good time unless Chester's having fun, too. And this is the first time I've actually wanted to go out with a guy since . . . you know."

Yeah. I knew. Stupid, lame, Jeremy. I sighed. Rach needed to date and get over her love slump. No matter how much I'd been looking forward to it, scheduling dates with my online prospects could wait a day. I swiveled in my chair to face my computer, then glanced over my shoulder at her eager face. "You owe me."

She squealed. "You're the best! I'm gonna go tell Gina."

"Yeah, yeah," I said, then smiled. Finally, she was excited about a guy again. Rach deserved an evening of fun.

As I returned to my report about the exorbitant amount Mr. Watson wanted for his computer crash, I couldn't help but remember that I was single, too. So, why had Gina asked Rach to go out with Mr. Muscles and not me?

LATER THAT NIGHT, I parked in front of Rachel's apartment in East Sacramento as my cell phone shrilled. I scanned the screen—*Mom*—then pressed the green button. "I can't talk. Anything important going on?"

"Just calling to see who you picked for the first date, sweetheart." Her voice held excitement. "The engineer or the entrepreneur?"

"Neither." I shut the door of my sedan and hurried up the cement walkway toward apartment 8A. "I got stuck late at work and Rachel has a hot date, so I'm babysitting her miniature beagle."

"Oh, is my darling Rachel finally over that Jeremy character? I had my suspicions about him ever since your cousin's play opening. He refused to look me in the eye when he shook my hand. Add that to your list of things to watch out for, Ellen. If they act shifty, they are shifty." She sighed. "If I'd known at your age half of what I do now . . . I never would've married Bob. Or, Frank, for that matter."

As I knocked on the brown door to Rachel's apartment, my brows furrowed. "Don't forget my dad."

"I never married him," she said, quickly. "So, that doesn't count."

My stomach clenched even though he really shouldn't count for much. I'd only met the man a handful of times myself. But, it's like her opinion was fact with no regard for how I felt. Story of my life. "Can I talk to you later?"

"Well, there's another thing I was calling about. Remember that art gallery opening Robert and I told you about last week? It's this Friday night and they're show-casing an up-and-coming artist. It's supposed to be fabulous. Any interest? Maybe you can invite one of your dates?"

"That's exactly how I want to meet a potential boyfriend for the first time." My voice held a teasing tone. "With my nosy mom and her new husband."

"It was worth a try." She chuckled. "Bring Rachel, then. We'll meet for dinner beforehand?"

Rachel's front door opened and I pointed toward my ear to indicate I was on the phone. "Sounds good. I'll call you tomorrow to find out where."

I told my mom I loved her, hung up, then sighed as I turned my attention to Rach. "My mom drains me."

She shrugged with one shoulder. "What else is new?"

"Very funny." I leaned forward for a quick hug. "Want to go to an art showing with my mom and Robert Friday night? Some new artist."

"Since you're my savior, absolutely." She gave me a

squeeze, then pulled the door shut behind us. "Chester is super excited to spend time with you."

I dropped my phone into my overflowing purse. "I'll look forward to my Auntie of the Year trophy."

"Definitely." Her heels clicked across the tiled floor as she strutted into the kitchen wearing dressy black pants, an electric blue silk top, and a whimsical smile.

"You look fantastic," I said, giving Chester a little pat as I walked past where he lay—in his doggy bed, chewing a rope toy (finally his vicious canines were sinking their teeth into something appropriate)—then followed her to the kitchen, wishing I were going on a date instead of dog sitting.

"Thanks." She smiled, her brown eyes lighting up. "His name's Dillon and we talked on the phone earlier. He has this really deep voice and sounds super nice."

I slipped onto one of her bar stools and leaned against the countertop. "It'd be better to have more info on him though. That's what I love about Detailed Dating. You learn what you're getting into before you invest time and energy."

"Only if the guys are honest in their profile. Do you know how many horror stories I've heard?"

"That's why it's only *part* of Detailed Dating's process. It's not like they recommend marrying someone off their profile alone." I laughed.

"Still, online dating feels too clinical to me." She fished in a drawer, then handed me an extendable leash that had a plastic handle with blue plastic bags attached. "I'm more into chemistry and a good vibe."

My mouth twisted. "Says the girl who's going out with some guy she's never met because he looks good without a shirt on."

"Touché."

I took a deep breath, but my voice still cracked a little when I said, "Why do you think Gina set you up with Dillon and not me?"

She leaned on the counter across from me and stared into my eyes. "Does that bug you?"

I shrugged, feeling rejected. "Maybe a little . . ."

She grasped my hands. "Sweetie, you've been raving about Detailed Dating for practically a month. She probably figures that's working for you whereas I'm a pathetic mess who needs help."

I wanted to laugh at her attempted joke, but my eyes filled with tears instead. Maybe Gina wasn't the reason I felt rejected.

Her hands tightened around my own. "Ellen, what's going on?"

My shoulders rose and my throat burned. "I'm not sure. I was talking to my mom earlier and she mentioned Bob, Frank . . . and my dad."

Her eyes grew large. "In what context?"

I blinked back tears and swiped at my nose. "Basically, she said how she screwed up with them and I shouldn't make the same mistake. It shouldn't bother me." Logically, I knew this. My dad had been absent most of my life and I didn't owe him one ounce of loyalty. "But she said that my dad didn't count. Since she hadn't married him, he didn't count."

Rachel leaned on her elbow and gave me a stern look. "Of course he counts. I'm sure it's just her way of getting over it. Since he left her and all."

"He left me, too. And I'm not the one who chose him. She did." My eyes burned and the hole in my chest ached. I shook my head. "She picked someone who didn't want kids, who wasn't compatible with her. When I marry, it has to be to a guy who's stable and in it for the long run. I have to know everything about him to make sure I choose someone who would never desert me. Ever."

She blew out a breath. "If we only had a crystal ball." Her lips tightened. "Then, I'd have seen Jeremy's true colors and not wasted two years of my life on that slime bag."

"Exactly," I said, wishing we could see the future and know if it would all work out. "All I can do is take every step possible to make sure we're compatible so it will last."

"Even so, you're not going to get a sealed guarantee," Rachel said, glumly.

Knock. Knock.

We both jumped as someone rapped on her front door. Dillon, no doubt.

Turning back to me, she said, "And with that cheery thought . . ."

"Sorry. I'm ruining your first date in six months." I groaned, then picked up Chester's leash off the counter and waved toward the front door. "Ignore my dark side and have fun. And don't worry about your mutt either. I'll keep him entertained."

She gave me a quick hug, started toward the door, then turned back. "I can cancel if you're upset."

"No way. I'm fine." I held up the leash. "Chester and I will go for a walk and get some fresh air."

"Thanks, Ellen. We'll find the right guy for us. Or, at least die trying." She winked at me, then opened the front door and greeted her hot date.

Unable to resist a peek, I leaned sideways to see if he looked as good in person as he did in his beach photo. Sandy-brown hair, broad build, and that dynamic smile. Ooh, baby.

After a polite exchange between them, the front door closed, and all was quiet in the apartment. Chester trotted over to the door with his tail high, sniffed at the weather strip, then started whining.

Once I heard car doors slam outside, I clipped the leash onto Chester's collar. He stopped whining, nudged my hand with his wet nose, and looked up at me expectantly.

"It's just you and me tonight, chew monster." I watched his brown ears prick up. "If you meet any pretty pups tonight, do me a favor. Don't romance them if you're not going to follow through. Being abandoned is no picnic."

Arf! Arf!

As Chester wagged his tail, my lips curved up slightly. His cheerful yips seemed to tell me not to worry. My mouth thinned when I realized this was what my life had come to. Getting advice on men from a four-month-old miniature beagle who, let's face it, hadn't exactly been around the block.

~

AFTER A TWENTY-MINUTE WALK, I arrived back at Rachel's apartment with her pint-sized dog who'd felt the need to lift his leg at practically every tree we passed. He'd even attempted to water a parked SUV's rear tire, but I'd managed to tug him away in time.

I shut the front door, unhooked Chester's leash from his collar, and dropped the apartment key onto the wooden entry table. Setting my purse on the arm of the couch, I searched through the mess for my phone while vowing, once again, to finally clean out my handbag. Right.

Once I located my cell, my stomach growled, so I raided Rachel's freezer. While waiting for my microwave dinner to "cook," I propped myself onto a barstool and unlocked the keypad on my phone. I slid my finger across the screen to see if I had any Detailed Dating emails. Oh, got one!

To: *smrt4ever*
From: *jusUnME*

Ellen,

I've enjoyed our discussions over the past few weeks and feel that you're both witty and intelligent—an ideal combination. On my end, we've progressed through Detailed Dating's "initial screen-ing" process, so if you're interested in the "face-to-face" part of DD's procedure, perhaps you are free for dinner tomorrow night? You've mentioned your affinity for chow mein, so I thought Wok N' Roll in Old Sac might be to your liking? Would seven-thirty work? Look forward to hearing from you.

— Craig

I GAZED at the humming microwave and considered his offer. Since I'd been planning on initiating the face-to-face, as well, that meant *jusUnME* and I were on the same page, just as I'd expected. I liked his take-charge-without-being-obnoxious ways, too. Guys who expect their girlfriend to plan everything? I'd pass. I prefer someone who could actu-ally pick up the phone to make dinner reservations and, if I'm really lucky, call the babysitter to watch our two kids. I'd been planning on suggesting a coffee date (easier for a fast getaway, if needed), but he'd chosen the restaurant based on our previous exchanges and my preferences. Another point in his favor, which made up my mind. The entrepreneur would be my first face-to-face!

To: *jusUnME*
From: smrt4ever

Craig,

Tomorrow night sounds fun. Thanks for giving in on our Chinese food debate. We'll make sure not to order anything spicy for you! Looking forward to dinner and I'll see you at seven-thirty.

Ellen

AFTER I HIT SEND, the microwave went *ding*. Perfect timing.

I eased off the chair, removed a plate from the cupboard, and opened the microwave door. The smell of alfredo sauce wafted up my nose. Yum.

Hagh! Hagh!

At the unusual noise, my head whipped toward the living room, eyes scanning the room for the source of the strange sounds.

Hagh! Hagh!

My eyes froze on the spot where Rachel's Snoopy-looking destroyer had apparently knocked over my purse— the contents dribbled from the arm of the couch, to the seat cushions, and onto the floor. The four-legged terror stood with his mouth wide as he continued making awful choking noises.

"Oh, no!" I ran over to Chester, who backed away, somehow managing to look guilty even as he hacked loudly. I grabbed my bag and searched for what he might've eaten. "What is wrong with you, dog? Have you no self-control?"

Hagh! Hagh!

In my purse, I pushed aside my wallet, hairbrush, and a bottle of aspirin, which I frantically examined . . . still capped, thank goodness. Various lip-glosses lay strewn across the couch, several canine-sized holes in the plastic tubes oozing various shades of pink onto the beige sofa. Could designer lip-gloss be toxic to dogs? I stared at Chester as he began foaming at the mouth.

My hands flew to the sides of my head, gripping my hair between my fingers. "Is he dying? What should I do?" My heart raced and I tried to take deep calming breaths to no avail. "Rachel's going to kill me!"

I couldn't call her, that's for sure. She would freak and we didn't have time for that. I had to act quickly. Who could help? Oh, wait. An animal doctor. Duh. I raced to the counter where I'd left my phone, and used my search app to locate the closest one.

Three blocks away. I could get there in time. At least I hoped.

"Hang on, Chester." I grabbed his leash, a kitchen towel, and what was left of my shredded handbag. "We're going to the vet."

~

A HAIR before 6:00 p.m., Chester and I rushed into All Things Furry. Ignoring the people in the waiting room—there was a surprising amount for a Monday evening—I raced to the counter, but nobody was behind it.

"Hello?!" I rang the metal bell obsessively. "I need help *please*. Emergency!"

Hagh-ech! Hagh-ech!

Holding Rachel's bright yellow dishtowel under Chester's saliva-dripping mouth, I panicked at the morphed sounds he was making. "Hang in there, dude."

I shifted him in my arms then slammed on the metal bell some more. "Does anyone work here?"

"Can I help?" A male voice came from behind me.

"Yes, this dog got into my purse and—" I paused mid-sentence as my gaze met dark gray eyes that sent a bolt of adrenaline through me. My heart flipped in my chest. Not an appropriate reaction when Rach's dog could be dying. "I-I think he ate something toxic. Maybe my lip-gloss? Are you the vet? Can you give him that charcoal stuff to make him barf it up?"

He studied Chester's half-open mouth. "Try setting him down. I'll take a look."

"Thanks." I knelt, still holding the towel under his mouth—because, *ew*, slobber all over the place.

The vet dropped to his knees next to Chester and pried his little jaw open.

Hech! Hech!

As he examined the dog's throat, I couldn't help checking *him* out. There was something going on behind those dark eyes that had me dying to learn everything about him. Where he was from, what made him tick, what he looked for in a girl...

My pulse slammed into overdrive.

Weird that the vet was wearing sweats, though. Maybe he'd finished with his last patient and was going for a run? Definitely looked like a guy who worked out regularly. Yeah, that's what I should be thinking about while my friend's dog was gagging for his life. What was *wrong* with me? Focus, Ellen. "Can you save him?"

"Hang on a sec." As Chester strained away from him, he reached his thumb and index finger down his throat. "I think I've found the culprit."

With both hands, I tried my best to hold the squiggly pup in place. Couldn't the dog understand we were trying to save his miniature beagle life?

From deep down Chester's throat, he pulled out a huge glob of wet, dirty-blond hair. Yuck.

"It looks prettier on your head," he said, a hint of laughter in his voice.

I cringed, wrapping the mangled hair into a napkin from my purse. "Uh, well..."

Okay, so I keep a hairbrush in my handbag. And I don't clean it regularly. How could I have known some freakoid dog would snack on it?

"I think you're gonna live." The guy rubbed a hand across the moronic pup's black, brown and white head. "What's his name?"

"Chester." Relieved that he was going to be fine, I

watched as the ungrateful animal wriggled away, lifted his hind foot, and scratched his ear without so much as a look of appreciation. "And yours is Dr . . .?"

"Henry." He reached out to shake my hand.

"I'm Ellen." When I slipped my hand into his firm grasp, my insides warmed. And, okay, I probably held on longer than I needed to. Snap out of it, girl. "You're the vet?"

"Me? No." He stood and brushed dog hair off his pants. "We're here for dog obedience school."

"We?" My heart sank and I scanned the room for his wife or girlfriend.

"Kenzie and me." He gestured toward the big black lab I hadn't noticed hiding under a chair. "Found her wandering by the side of the freeway last month. She was skin and bones. I called the local shelters and checked the newspaper, but nothing. Someone must've dumped her."

"That's too bad." Her weight seemed healthy now, thanks to her new owner. Compassionate and perhaps single? No ring, but he could be dating someone. Or two someones. Or five. Too many unanswered questions. Despite my attraction to him, I reminded myself why I'd signed up for Detailed Dating. So they could ask all the hard questions and I would have the answers. All I had to do was check a guy's profile to see if he was A) single and dating; B) single and looking for an exclusive relationship; C) single and looking for a casual relationship (aka: hookups). Meeting a cute guy on my own left too many unknowns to stress over. Time to go. "Well, thank you so much for your help, Henry."

"Anytime." He seemed to take my hint, nodded, then went over to Kenzie (who nuzzled his leg as soon as he sat down in the leather chair).

I found his pup's cuddling adorable. The dog had been scared stiff a moment ago, but obviously felt safe with Henry.

I'd been the one to cut our conversation short, but the distance between us suddenly felt wrong. When I realized I was standing in the middle of the room all by myself, I felt lame. So, I started toward the door and then realized I didn't have Chester with me. I quickly scanned the room. No! No! No!

First, I'd nearly killed him. Now, I'd *lost* him. Rachel had way too much faith in my dog-sitting abilities.

"He's over there." A white-haired woman with a poodle on her lap pointed toward a potted plant in the corner of the room. Chester was gnawing on one of its leaves.

A little boy near the front door snickered. "Your dog totally needs obedience school."

"That's not polite, Junior." His mother scrunched up her nose, the expression implying she agreed with her son but wasn't going to say it.

It annoyed me that the woman had judged my friend's dog. Especially because she was correct in her assessment. But, that wasn't the spoiled beagle's fault. Like the kid said, the poor mutt had never been trained.

"Come on, Chester." As I tugged him away from the plant, the back door opened.

A young blonde wearing pink velour sweatpants with a

matching zip-up hoodie stepped into the lobby, checking her clipboard. "Good evening, everyone. I'm Abby Wilson, and welcome to Simply Skilled. I take it you're all here for dog obedience class?"

Affirmations sounded throughout the room, and one in particular stood out. Hearing Henry's voice tugged at something inside me.

I raised my hand. "Is it too late to sign up?"

GLANCING around the waiting room at the gold-framed puppy and kitten pictures in All Things Furry, I could see why Abby Wilson had charged me an insane amount of money to enroll Rachel's canine tornado in Simply Skilled obedience class. This vet clinic appeared to be hosting the Cambridge of doggy schools. In today's dismal economy, it was hard to believe they'd managed to pack the place. Even harder to believe, I'd made a significant financial decision on a whim. But, there was a mystery behind those deep gray eyes that I needed to solve...

Clearly, I was not in my right mind.

As Abby ran my credit card, I stole a glance at Henry who smiled at me. I shrugged and said, quietly, "He obviously needs it."

I signed the slip Abby handed me, then skimmed through the glossy brochure she'd included with my receipt. In addition to dogs, they train all kinds of hairy creatures. Apparently if you want your hamster to put his paws on his glass wall and wave to you, this was the place to come.

Ruff. Ruff. Chester jumped up against my shins and wagged his Snoopy tail as though thanking me for his first doggy class. That, or he felt stoked for another opportunity to eat something he shouldn't. We'd see if this class could cure him of that urge.

Abby strode to the center of the room and told us her résumé. Although I could feel Henry's gaze on me, I kept my eyes glued to the perky woman and tried to play it cool. Because, hello? I'd just met the guy and already I'd blown a designer pair of shoes' worth of moola because I was wondering if Henry had felt the same—what had Rachel called it?—*chemistry* and *vibe* that I did with him.

Abby clapped her hands and threw a fist in the air. "When we leave at the end of the four-day session this week, your beloved pet will understand the basic commands: sit, stay, and heel. Plus, on Thursday, our last day together, we'll work on a special individual skill of your choice that you want your furry friend to master."

All I wanted to master was more time with Henry. Although getting this mutt to stop eating my stuff would be an awesome side benefit.

Abby's blonde ponytail bobbed as she waved her hand over her shoulder. "Let's come on back and get started."

Out of the corner of my eye, I saw Henry rise from his chair. I slyly waited for the dozen others in the room to follow her first so I could bring up the rear with him.

His face was somber as we fell into step together. "Give

me a call if you need me to save your dog from deadly hair again."

My belly danced at his adorable flirtation. "That's very kind of you, but he's not mine. He belongs to my best friend." I glanced at Chester who was sniffing Kenzie's, uh, private region. So rude! "I'm hoping to win an Auntie of the Year award by being the world's best dog sitter."

"Tough start with the choking thing," he said, while managing a straight face.

"You have no evidence of that." I nudged his elbow, playfully. "I've been Rachel's friend for more than four years. She would never believe your word over mine."

"She go out of town?" he said, as we entered a large room with an arena made out of bright green sod.

I shook my head. "Out on a hot date."

He gave me a curious look. "She gets a hot date and you're left watching her dog?"

"Doesn't seem fair, does it?" Although, the way we were flirting almost made me feel like I was on a date, too. Too bad this class didn't include wine by the fireplace.

Kenzie whimpered, and I looked down to find Chester nuzzling her with his nose. "He really does believe he owns the world. Think this class will teach him anything?"

He studied me for a moment with those deep gray eyes. "I think it'll be worth our time."

I couldn't wait to see if that statement turned out to be true.

CHAPTER TWO

THE NEXT DAY, I couldn't help but agree with Henry. The class had definitely been worth my time—and the money I'd paid. But that was my hormones talking. I told myself to be more practical, even as the man on the phone, Gilbert Watson, gave me an earful on how our financial software program was to blame for his computer woes.

"Sir, if you would listen to me—" I tried interjecting, but he talked over me trying to talk over him.

"My laptop worked perfectly before. Now, it's slow. Sometimes it even shuts down on me. Big business is out to screw the innocent, unsuspecting consumer and I will stand up for my rights. My wife totally agrees with me about this!" he said.

Considering I didn't know his wife, that really didn't matter, but as he took a breath, I jumped in, hoping to chill the man out. "We're a *small* business, Mr. Watson, and I assure you—"

No use. The dude had zero interest in a two-way conversation. He wanted to vent. As a customer service rep, I should be fine with this but, after only two hours of sleep, I was *not* in an emotional place to hear his diatribe on the evils of capitalism. And I hadn't spent the remaining six hours of my night tossing and turning with thoughts of Chester in my head. No, I'd been obsessing about the guy who'd saved him.

When I'd gone to bed at ten o'clock, I'd snuggled into my pillow and pictured the way Henry Holbrook III (I'd managed to find out his full name, if nothing else) had smiled at me every time I'd made a joke during dog school. Normally I took class, any kind of class, seriously. I'm an A student (fine, A-/B+). But yesterday evening, all I could pay attention to was Henry. And that had been true even after I'd gone to bed. Actually, it had been *more* true.

Then I'd thought about my date with Craig and reminded myself I hardly knew anything about who Henry really was. More importantly, I didn't know if we were compatible. I mean, he had a dog and I didn't. I'd never owned any kind of animal, actually. Hairy things shed a lot and I kept my town home immaculate. Did *he* own a home? Did he live in the area? If so, did he plan to stay in this area? What did he do for a living? And did he like to travel?

If my mom's marriage history had taught me anything, it was that relationships won't last if your life goals and interests aren't in line. Everyone knows the more conflict, the more arguing. I'd heard my mom and Hubby Number

One get into heated discussions repeatedly and, not a shocker, they had zilch in common.

I mean, did I want to end up like my mother? Mentally deleting her child's father from her love list? Absolutely not. If she'd done her proper homework, she would've known he didn't want kids—and that one should always double-up on birth control.

"Mr. Watson?" I managed to get out when he'd paused for a breath. "Why don't you bring your laptop to our office and I'll have our service guys take a look at it. Free of charge. Okay?"

It wasn't the thousands of dollars he wanted for a new laptop, but it was all I could do. Thankfully, he accepted. After listing his agenda for the week (a doctor appointment Tuesday, taking the car in for an oil change Wednesday, and a waxing appointment on Thursday—I didn't ask the details and really didn't want to know), we agreed that he would come into the office before lunch on Friday.

I hung up the phone, dropped my head on the desk, and moaned.

"Tough phone call?" Gina stood in the doorway of my work cubicle.

I rolled my head toward her so that my ear was on my forearm. "Tough night, tough call, tough *everything*."

"That's deep." She came up next to me, leaned her petite frame against the small filing cabinet by my desk, and gestured toward the cube next to me. "So, I guess you're not in the mood to hear about Rachel and Dillon then?"

That had me sitting up fast. "I left her apartment after ten last night and she still wasn't home." I wiggled a finger in the direction of my adjacent cubicle. "And obviously she hasn't come into work yet . . ."

"Don't get ahead of yourself." Gina put a hand on my arm and leaned toward me, conspiratorially. "Dillon was the perfect gentleman. Rach just overslept from staying out late."

"So . . .?"

Gina came over and fiddled with one of my many Detailed Dating pens, seemed lost in thought for a few moments, then shook her head as if to snap out of whatever she'd been thinking. "The Oasis had a new band playing last night and they totally rocked. George and I hung out with them until almost midnight when Dillon and Rachel went out for coffee. And according to George, Dillon didn't get home until after two."

"Wow." I hadn't pegged Mr. Beach Hottie as a big conversationalist. "Good for Rach."

"Yeah." Gina set the cherry-red pen back on my desk and gave me a sad look. "Watch it work out between them. They could be married before George even proposes."

My heart went out to her since it really did seem like George was proposal-challenged. "Gina, talk to him. Ask him where it's going."

"I have. Maybe it's time again." She gave a forced smile. "How are things in the Detailed Dating world?"

"Great," I said, mentally reminding myself I was

supposed to be excited about my *face-to-face* tonight. "I'm taking Rachel's pooch to doggy class after work, then I'm meeting one of the guys for dinner."

Gina raised an eyebrow. "You're taking Chester to dog class? Why?"

The image of deep gray eyes framed with dark lashes popped into my head, but I ignored that and lifted my foot onto my desk. "See what her mutt did?"

Gina glanced at the marked-up boot and shook her head. "Ouch. Those were cute, too."

My mouth turned down. "I'm determined to get my money's worth out of them."

"That's big of you to take Chester to obedience school, but I have to say I think it's a lost cause." She paused, probably thinking the same thing I was. That George was a lost cause, too. "Well, I'd better get back to my desk. Have fun on your date."

"Thanks." I waved to her, then turned to my computer, and pulled up the Detailed Dating website. A few keystrokes, plus the click of my mouse, and a picture of Craig displayed on the screen.

He was a handsome man, for sure. Plus, we both liked skiing, boating, traveling, wanted at least two kids or maybe three, had similar political views, and sounded compatible.

So, why was I more into taking Rachel's pampered pup to All Things Furry than a date I'd been screening for almost six weeks? Intense chemistry shouldn't trump compatibility if I wanted a lasting relationship, which I did.

I closed out the screen, drafted a message to our

service department setting up Gilbert Watson's appointment on Friday, and hit SEND so hard the key nearly broke.

I would not make the same mistakes my mom had with my dad and pick a guy just because he made me go weak in the knees. No, I wanted a marriage that would last for life, which meant choosing a guy who makes the most sense logically. Tonight, I'd enjoy my first *face-to-face*—even if it killed me.

I RAPPED my knuckles on Rachel's apartment door half an hour before the Simply Skilled class started.

Rachel's front door flew open and she stared at me. "I got your message that you're coming to pick Chester up. What gives?"

"Nothing." Since I couldn't make sense of my irrational feelings, I so didn't want to talk about them with her. "I just want to borrow your dog. Is that so wrong? Chester? Come here, little poochie."

Rach blocked my path with her arm. "Last week you didn't even know his name. I'm officially scared."

"Aha!" Her little maniac was curled up by the heating vent on a bone-shaped doggy bed. His big, brown eyes widened as I approached. "Auntie's going to take you to obedience class. Yes, I am."

Rachel knelt down protectively over her dog. "This is about my going on a date with Dillon. Isn't it? You're feeling left out because Gina asked me instead and so you've snapped."

"Pfft. You think I want that six-one, surfing-dude who looks like he works out twelve hours a day? You can have him." I brushed my hand through the air. "You know me, I'm not competitive."

"Says the girl who nearly took my hand off at the company picnic four and a half years ago."

"It was the last piece of cake and I saw it first," I shot back. "Maybe I just want to teach your mutt some manners. Lest he try to munch on any more of my shoes."

"But," Rachel stammered. "You hate dogs."

Remembering the way Kenzie had nuzzled up to her rescuer's leg, my mouth dropped open indignantly. "I do not."

She stared at me and I stared back. She kept her eyes on mine and turned her head suspiciously. I mirrored her look.

Then she gasped. "You met someone who signed up for this dog class. Didn't you? Fess up."

My body froze. "No. I, uh . . ."

"You are using my sweet baby as a man magnet!" She gestured toward Chester, who nearly jumped off his bone bed when she shouted.

"For your information, I took your crazy woofer to the emergency vet yesterday because I thought he was dying!"

Her face went white and she threw her hand over her heart. "What?"

Oops. Wrong thing to say. "It wasn't my fault, all right?

He attacked my purse while I was heating up my dinner. He ate almost everything in it, including those new lip-glosses I bought at the mall the other day that the sales lady said went perfectly with my fair complexion."

"And he nearly died? You were supposed to be *watching* him."

"Funny story," I said, though I seriously doubted she'd laugh. "I took him to All Things Furry and the vet wasn't there because it was after hours. But there was this guy who was waiting for doggy school who has these amazing eyes I can't stop thinking about and, well, he found a clump of hair in Chester's throat. From my hairbrush. So, it turned out he wasn't dying. Just coughing on a hairball. See? No harm at all. Won't that be a funny story to tell the grandpups?"

"Chester's neutered." She didn't laugh, but she seemed to relax a little. "Tell me about this guy with the scintillating eyes. I assume he's the reason for your newfound interest in my sweet baby?"

I'd been caught. It was time to come clean. "His name's Henry Holbrook III."

She blinked at me. "And?"

"He is all I can think about." I stared blankly at the leash in my hand. "It's absurd, Rach. Absolutely ridiculous. I know nothing about him except that he adopted some stray dog who could have had rabies for all he knew. I mean, who does that?"

Silence.

I looked up at my best friend, begging for some

wisdom. She knew me better than anyone. She'd get me back on track. "This is the complete opposite of Detailed Dating. It doesn't go with my plan. You have to help me. What should I do?"

Rachel leaned forward with a serious look. "I think you should go for it."

And then she handed me her dog.

CHAPTER THREE

IT WAS illogical to feel so strongly about some random guy I'd only met once, but when I spotted Henry getting off his bike in front of All Things Furry, butterflies fluttered in my tummy. The fluttering stopped abruptly, however, when I noticed he was wearing the same sweats he had on yesterday. My blood ran cold.

Either (1) he hadn't changed clothes since yesterday (*ew*); (2) he was wearing different sweats that looked exactly the same (*lack of creativity*); or (3) he'd taken off the sweats and been naked doing . . . something . . . and had put the sweats back on since he hadn't had another set of clothes at wherever he'd stayed (*shoot me now*).

He locked his bike and his mouth curved upward when he saw Chester and me approaching. "Hi, Ellen. Chester."

"Hi." I smiled back, so happy that he'd remembered my name that I momentarily forgot to be concerned about the sweats. Then I noticed dark circles under his eyes and my mouth went flat. Tired? Same outfit? He'd obviously stayed at his girlfriend's place, had fun all night with her, and hadn't had time to change outfits. My stomach sank, but I tried not to let it show. "Late night?"

May as well ask and take the dagger to my heart now.

He rubbed a hand over his face. "It shows, huh?"

"Hmm." Frustrated that his response didn't give me a clue what he'd been doing, I tried again. "Was it at least fun?"

He appeared deep in thought. "It was . . . intense."

What did that mean? "But in a good way I hope."

Kenzie peered between his legs and he patted her head. "Time will tell."

"Huh." The guy had a knack for vague. I loosened my grip on Chester's leash so he could bump noses with Kenzie, who had her jaw to the ground. She stared at his invasive snout suspiciously.

"Before I forget . . ." Henry reached into his pocket and pulled out a bright red pen covered with bumpy hearts and handed it to me. "You left this here last night."

My cheeks heated at the Detailed Dating inscription. "How'd you know it was mine?"

He opened the front door and gestured for us to go through first. "Abby gave it to me after class. Said you left it when you signed your credit card slip."

Stunned by the knowledge that he'd been with Abby after class, I swallowed my dry throat. Was she the reason he'd had so little sleep? If so, why hadn't she returned the pen to me herself? "Oh, uh, thanks."

"No problem." He followed us inside and took a seat in the chair next to me.

Trying to delete the disturbing mental image of Henry and our beautiful blonde obedience instructor together, I studied the people around the room. The boy from yesterday had his eyes focused on an electronic device as his thumbs worked the buttons furiously. His mom sat next to him, flipping the pages of a magazine. Then I caught the elderly lady with the poodle eyeing Henry and me knowingly.

Yeah. I wish, lady.

"How's that working out for you, Ellen?"

Confused, I turned toward Henry's inquisitive voice that Abby had probably gotten to hear intimately. "Huh?"

He gestured toward my purse. "The online dating."

"Fine." I cleared my throat, suddenly annoyed that he'd been so friendly to me in class yesterday when he'd really been interested in Abby Wilson. "Very well, actually. I have a date tonight that I'm really looking forward to."

Okay, did my voice sound as defensive to him?

He opened his mouth to say something when Abby burst out of the back room clapping her hands. "Welcome to the second class of Simply Skilled, everyone!"

His mouth closed and he turned toward the beautiful woman who was wearing baby blue velour sweats that showed off her curves. Quite the opposite of my flower-print button-up blouse and khaki pants, which were flattering and pretty in a more understated way.

I wondered painfully what Henry had been about to

say. Did he care that I had a date with another man tonight? Had that made him as jealous as I felt over Abby Wilson?

I hoped so. But, it was impossible to tell his thoughts from the blank look on his face.

Chester's tail thumped against my leg as everyone got up to follow Abby to the back room. I forced myself to stand and was surprised to find Henry waiting for me.

"Is your friend Rachel on another date tonight?"

I shrugged. "Not sure what her plans are."

"Ah." He nodded. "You're volunteering on your own tonight, huh? Still going for that Auntie of the Year award?"

I took a step forward but my hand jerked backward when the leash resisted, so I checked behind me. Chester, it turned out, was smacking his mouth like he'd just licked something off the floor that had stuck to his tongue. Gross.

"Something like that." I shook my head at the canine garbage disposal. Was there anything this mutt wouldn't put in his mouth?

Henry waited for Chester and me to go through the doorway of the training arena. As he followed us inside, I purposefully picked the spot farthest from our bouncy instructor. To my surprise, Henry and Kenzie chose the spot to the right of us.

"Yesterday, you taught your dog how to sit." Abby's voice rang out enthusiastically, her facial expressions animated. "Today, you're going to teach him or her to stay, and only to come when you ask. Let me demonstrate."

She asked for a volunteer and a young guy with a bulldog offered right away. Probably had a crush on her, too. Admittedly, Abby was gorgeous—if you were into physical perfection, that is.

But was she organized? Because a man would be hard-pressed to find a woman more organized than me. I mean, my checking account is balanced to the penny, my glass shower door never has a streak, and my unmatched sock basket is practically non-existent (no, I won't toss the loner socks because their mates will surely turn up the day after I do).

Any chance Henry considers Type-A to be the new sexy? Could be possible. . .

As Abby waxed poetic about well-mannered pooches, I leaned toward Henry, determined to get to the bottom of his mysterious nocturnal activities. "Abby looks exceptionally pretty today. Don't you think?"

He looked uncomfortable at the question. "I guess."

Okay, that confirmed nothing about his night. Or, maybe it did. If they'd hooked up, he would have agreed a bit more enthusiastically. Right? The curiosity was killing me. "She seems very nice, too."

My stomach tightened as I braced for his answer because I only needed to know if he was into her, not any of the details.

"She does." He continued to watch Abby as she made the bulldog stay with a flat hand signal. "Although, this is my first dog obedience class, so I don't really have another instructor to compare her to."

The knot in my belly loosened. It was unlikely he'd talk that distantly about her if they'd been up all night doing, well, everything I'd fantasized doing with Henry if I had him all to myself.

Slightly mollified, I stole another glance at the circles under Henry's eyes. They hadn't been there yesterday. Believe me, I'd studied every detail of his beautiful face and had gone over it a thousand times in my mind. The stubble hadn't been there either. What had he been doing that he couldn't shave or change his clothes? And that, in his own words, was intense?

Everyone around me suddenly started moving. Apparently Abby had instructed us to do something. I'd been paying zero attention, so I mimicked what other people were doing by commanding Chester to "sit" and then holding my hand up horizontally and telling him to "stay."

It was an honest miracle that the mutt obeyed. For about two seconds anyway. Then he turned his head to the side, and started whining.

I stared at the pedigree pup, wondering what his problem was. Oh, great. He'd better not have to use the restroom. I'd seen the blue plastic bags attached to the handle of his leash, but I'd been hoping I'd never have to use them. "What, boy?"

He whined some more and then barked at me.

I cringed. Half an hour with the miniature male and already I wasn't meeting his needs. If he weren't attached to my leash, he'd probably ditch me. "Why are you staring at me like that?"

"He's waiting for a treat." Henry sounded amused as he

broke a brown, bone-shaped biscuit in half and held it out for me between his fingertips. "Here . . ."

When had they handed out dog treats? Oh, right. While I'd been tormenting myself on Henry's whereabouts last night even though we were clearly not compatible. I mean, how many questions do I have to ask before the guy indicates if he's single or not? Not that it mattered since I had a date scheduled with a compatible man who, I might add, is up front about who he is and not dark and mysterious, with unforgettable dark pooled eyes. . .

"Thanks." I coached myself not to ask outright what he'd been doing all night long (without me) because it might show I was interested, and how would that look after I'd bragged about my date tonight?

"No worries." Henry smiled, seeming unaware of his effect on me. "This should be good for his size."

When I took the treat from him, our fingers brushed and my skin sizzled where we'd touched. Was that static electricity or . . . what?

I realized I was still holding my hand in the air and, uh, gaping at him. Not exactly sly there, Ellen. My cheeks went up in flames. See, I never had these problems using Detailed Dating. It was all behind the computer and . . . safe. Quickly, I turned back to Chester who was stomping his foot and staring at my hand with a starved expression. So impatient! "Here, boy."

I tossed the treat at him. Instead of catching it in his mouth like I'd expected, the cookie hit his nose and then bounced toward the black lab sitting next to him. When the bone landed by Kenzie's foot, growling ensued.

"Kenzie, heel." Henry used a firm voice but instead of listening, as man's best friend should, she opened jaws twice the size of Chester's and engulfed the cookie.

Grrr. Grrr. Chester crouched—not a happy camper.

"Sorry." I pulled Chester away from the treat-stealing dog since, let's face it, if Kenzie grew a backbone she could easily pummel Rachel's pup.

"I'm the one who should be sorry. My girl has no manners when it comes to dog biscuits." He pulled out another treat and handed it to me. "I guess that's why we're here, right?"

Uh, no. I was here because I couldn't stand the thought of leaving All Things Furry and never seeing this beautiful man again. When our fingers brushed, I had the urge to curl my hand into his. So *not* a good idea. "Thanks."

This time I held the treat close to Chester's mouth. He took it quickly and crunched it with a smug expression as his nemesis licked her lips and whined.

To avoid further embarrassment, I tried to pay attention the rest of class. My belly danced every time Henry made a joke or came close to me, and I found myself being playful back. I'd never felt comfortable enough to be silly in front of guys before, so why with Henry? Why did having fun with him feel so natural?

I had to keep reminding myself that I had a date tonight that I was supposed to be excited about.

WHEN I DROPPED Chester off at Rachel's apartment, she asked how class had gone. Even though I had the urge to tell my best friend everything, I stuck with, "Fine."

What can I say? My unprompted feelings for Henry Holbrook III, who I still knew almost nothing about, were totally embarrassing. And my obsession over Henry's unknown nocturnal activities? Pathetic. I couldn't admit them to Rachel.

I received a raised eyebrow, but was grateful she left it at that.

So, I drove to Old Sacramento and parked on the third floor of the brick encased parking garage. As I walked into Wok N' Roll at half-past seven o'clock, I was determined to remember that compatibility (not uncertainty) was the key to a lasting relationship.

I immediately spotted Craig in the waiting area. He had a nice smile, looked as handsome as his online photo, and seemed genuinely happy to see me. All things to check off my list.

Standing, he greeted me with a handshake. "So good to finally meet you in person, Ellen."

"Thanks. You, too."

"Should we have the waiter seat us?" he said, politely.

"That sounds great." I smiled, then watched appreciatively as he went up to the podium and had us escorted to a corner booth.

Craig was pleasant, polite, and a solid choice. Exactly

what I was looking for. I breathed a sigh of relief. It felt good to be back in my comfort zone.

After browsing the menu, we ordered several dishes to split, and then I sat back in my seat. "I can't wait to hear what you think of Chinese food. It's hard to believe you've never tried it."

He set his hands on the table, laced his fingers together, then met my gaze with a considerate expression. "I'm not as adventurous as I'd like to be when it comes to trying different cuisine. Which is not to say I'm close minded or not interested in other ethnicities." He cleared his throat. "It's just that I tend to go to the same restaurants and order dependable items on the menu. Not because something else might not be good or even better, but because I won't be disappointed. Does that make sense?"

I blinked. In all the dates I'd ever been on, I'd have to say that I'd never met a man that communicated this well. It was refreshing. "It makes a lot of sense. Thanks for sharing."

He seemed relieved. "I'm glad you understand. I'll admit my affinity for repetition has been a bit of a problem for me in the past, but it's something I've recently come to realize is a flaw and I am working on it."

"Um, okay." My eyes widened and I had the sudden feeling I'd invaded his private therapy session. "So, we agree. Chinese is good. Trying new things can be . . . good."

And conversation had taken a nosedive. . .

"It's invigorating to talk to a woman who is empathetic." He pulled out a little notepad from his pocket and crossed something off. "I feel that empathy is important in a relationship. Don't you?"

"I think so. I mean, yes. I suppose . . ." Had he scratched the word "empathy" off a check list? I wanted to snag his pad and see what else he had on there.

The waiter brought our dishes to the table and Craig nodded and thanked him. I smiled, murmured an appreciative remark, and then Craig drew another line across his pad.

So far Craig was an excellent communicator, had good manners, and apparently had some kind of list he was keeping to . . . what? Rate our date?

"Allow me." He scooped servings of chow mein, kung pao chicken, and fried rice onto our plates. Then he placed a napkin in his lap, picked up his fork in lieu of the chopsticks, and took a tentative bite of his noodles. "Interesting texture. Different flavor, but all in all, very pleasing."

"Hmm." I stuffed a forkful of chow mein into my mouth, considered an evaluation of my own, and came up with nothing. It was Chinese food, after all. Not a work of art.

He swallowed and gestured with his fork. "What do you think?"

I'd never been to Wok N' Roll before, but it tasted like normal Chinese food to me. "It's good."

"Okay." He nodded, then moved his head back and forth as if in thought. "How would you say it compares to other Chinese restaurants you've been to? Is this pretty average? Or exceptional, perhaps? If I were going to try another Chinese restaurant, would the chow mein taste similar to this one or does Wok N' Roll have their own spin on the dish?"

"Come on, Craig. I'm a customer service rep, not a professional food critic." I started to laugh, then realized he wasn't joining in. Oops, cracking jokes must've carried over from doggy class and weren't flying as well here.

"I know you're not a food critic. You work for a software company." His voice held a defensive tone. "But, I value your opinion and you certainly have more experience than I do in this area."

Why did chow mein have to be a serious topic? But, that should be fine. Right? I mean, he asked my opinion because he valued my thoughts. Even though he's known me all of twenty minutes. Well, plus a month or so of email exchanges. And, wouldn't most women find it gratifying to have a man communicate this much? I mean, how many times had my girlfriends and I complained that men never say what they're thinking? And here Craig was actually doing it.

So, why was it so freaking annoying?

I set my fork down and leaned forward. "I'd say it's average chow mein. It's good, has all the right stuff, but I've had better."

"Really? Where?" His notepad was in his hand again. "I'll be sure to take you there next time."

Next time? We weren't even done with this time, but I gave him the name and directions to my favorite Chinese restaurant downtown. Then, I vowed to chill through the rest of the meal because he really was a nice guy.

At the end of the date, he walked me to my car and asked me out for Thursday. I accepted. So, the guy had a list. I did, too. And he was meeting all of my compatibility requirements, so what kind of hypocrite would I be if I didn't go out with him a second time?

Still, something nagged at me and I couldn't figure out what. I guess that's why I went home, logged onto the Detailed Dating website and sent the following email to my second dating prospect:

To: *lookn4luv*
From: *smrt4ever*

Geoff,

Judging by our emails over the past month, we sound very compatible. Would you like to meet for coffee tomorrow night?

~ Ellen (aka: smrt4ever)

LESS THAN TEN MINUTES LATER, I got the following reply:

To: *smrt4ever*

From: *lookn4luv*

Hi Ellen!

Name the time and place. I'll set a red rose on the table so you'll be sure to recognize me. Looking forward to it.

— Geoff

ME TOO, I'd written back. Wishing it was really true.

In my mind, what I was really wishing for was a date with Henry.

CHAPTER FOUR

THE NEXT EVENING, Chester and I walked into All Things Furry just before six. The place was packed, as usual. My eyes scanned the room until they landed on Henry's. Even though I told myself he was all wrong for me, my tummy did a little dance.

Henry smiled and gestured to the chair next to him as if it were natural that we'd sit together.

I joined him, secretly thrilled he'd saved a seat for me. Kenzie hid behind Henry's legs, but peeked out to look at me. "Hi, Kenzie."

I reached my hand out slowly, but she ducked back under the chair. "It's okay, girl."

"Don't take it personally." He nudged my knee with his own. "The only way she'll come to my grandpa is if he has food in his hand."

Henry appeared exhausted again, but I jumped on the

opportunity to learn more about him. "Do you visit your grandfather often?"

"We pop by several times a week." He ran his hand under Kenzie's muzzle. "See what he and Gran are up to."

So sweet! My heart melted a little more. "You must be close."

He nodded. "As close as we can get, since they raised me."

The air felt heavy between us. "And your parents . . .?"

He continued rubbing Kenzie as he spoke, "They died in a car crash when I was six."

A chill ran through me. "I'm sorry to hear that."

"Thanks." His gaze flicked to mine, his dark eyes stormy with emotion. "Do your parents live nearby?"

I'd gone from knowing nothing about Henry to discovering what was probably the biggest tragedy of his life. We'd sped from zero to sixty in under a minute and I didn't know how to downshift, so I replied, "My mom lives about twenty minutes away in Land Park. My dad has been nonexistent since my college graduation. He wasn't around much before that either."

My chest ached, as it did any time I talked about my dad. One of the many reasons why I rarely did.

His gaze held mine, telling me that he understood the pain I felt. "You and your mom are close?"

"Too close." I laughed. "She's constantly causing me to go over my cell phone minutes. Guess I need to up my plan. I'll add that to my To Do list."

He winked at me. "Along with cleaning out your hairbrush."

I loved his teasing. "My purse is sacred. It's the one place I allow chaos in my life." I leaned my shoulder into his jokingly. "Besides, Chester took care of that for me already, remember?"

"Yes." His face grew serious. "I remember."

Although the room was crowded with chatter, everything fell silent as if the two of us were alone with a physical cord pulling us together. In a few sentences, it felt like we'd shared everything. The feeling overwhelmed me.

"Evening, everyone!" Abby marched out in red velour sweats and her blonde hair tumbled over her shoulders. "Great to see you all. Let's hit the arena."

Although Abby's cheery voice rang throughout the room, Henry kept his gaze on mine. "Ready?"

It felt like a loaded question and I answered it honestly. "Not in the slightest."

AFTER CLASS ENDED, Henry and I chatted outside about the pups and what they were learning (Kenzie coming out of her shell; Chester, not a thing). I had to tear myself away since I, uh, had a real date I was supposed to be on in a few minutes.

I rushed to drop Chester off so I wouldn't be late meeting *lookn4luv* at the coffee shop. Geoff and I had emailed again a couple of times to clarify timing and how to recognize each other. Although I saw the red rose lying across a bistro table as agreed, the man sitting there wasn't *lookn4luv*. It was a guy who could possibly be *lookn4luv's* distant not-as-good-looking cousin, but why would he be here? Maybe Geoff couldn't make it and sent his relative to tell me? Which would be pretty, you know, odd...

I approached the table slowly. "Hello?"

His head jerked up from his cell phone screen. "Wow! You're even prettier in person, Ellen."

My brows drew together in confusion. "And you are, who?"

"Geoff Bent." He stood, shook my hand, then gestured for me to take a seat. "I know what you're thinking, but let me explain. First, these are for you."

Keeping my purse on my shoulder, I dropped into the wooden bistro chair as the man claiming to be Geoff handed me a dozen red roses. "Thanks, uh, Geoff."

Due to the sadly hopeful look on his face, I accepted the bouquet even though it dawned on me that he'd falsified his photo.

"You're welcome." He flushed, bowed his head, then met my eyes. "The picture I posted on Detailed Dating is actually of me, I swear. I just used a photo editor to make myself look more how a woman would want me to."

Okay, his admission tugged at my sympathetic side. It did. But, I wasn't going to let him off the hook. "You've covered the way you think a date would want you to *look*, but how *honest* would she want you to be?"

He looked confused. "I don't follow you."

"There's zero chance of this going anywhere. Any possibility went out the window when you put up that phony photo." I watched his shoulders slump. "A good relationship can't come out of deceit."

His brows came together. "But, I'd never get a date with a girl like you otherwise."

I thought of Henry, his beautiful gray eyes, and my insides warmed. Admittedly, every girl probably wouldn't find him as sexy as I did. He didn't have that model look like Dillon that made him universally hot, but I felt so attracted to him it was hard to think straight. Surely, someone would feel that way about the man across from me.

"That's an absolute and total copout, Geoff." I stabbed my index finger on the table as I made my point. "Besides, why would you want to be with someone who wouldn't want to be with the real you?"

The look on his face told me he'd never considered that.

"You could be a nice guy. In fact, you probably are." I sighed, tightened my doggy-mangled purse on my shoulder, and stood. "So, I'll give you some free advice. Put up an authentic photo of yourself, be honest with any potential date, and don't settle for someone who doesn't want you for exactly who you are."

He nodded to me. "I'll try. Thanks, Ellen."

"You're welcome." The last of my irritation melted away and I turned to leave. "Best of luck."

"Before you go, can I buy you a coffee?" When I gave him a skeptical look, he raised his palms. "Just as friends?"

Deciding he was a decent guy with a few insecurities, I sat back down. "Sure."

Geoff ordered at the counter, returned to the table, and began fiddling with his stir straw. He appeared lost in thought as he twirled it again and again.

I sipped my latte and the hot liquid rolled down my throat. "Something wrong?"

"What you said before? About a person liking me for who I am?" He bent the straw, then straightened. "There's this girl. My neighbor, actually." A smile played at his lips. "I've been wanting to ask her out for a while, but my brother thinks she's out of my league . . ."

Nice sibling. No wonder Geoff was insecure. "Really?"

"I think about her a lot."

"Do you think she likes you back?" My voice had an encouraging tone. "You know, likes you exactly the way you are?"

"I'm not sure. She offered to help me with my laundry last week. Yesterday, she stopped by to see if I needed anything from the store. She smiles a lot."

"Sounds like she's got it bad for you." Wait . . . he liked her and she felt the same, but he didn't ask her out? It made no sense. "Don't let your brother's negativity influence you. Ask her out."

He fingered his straw. "But Sean, my brother, fell hard for a girl last year. When he built up the guts to ask her on a date, she laughed in his face. It crushed him."

"Wow. That's a shame," I said, thinking how brutal that girl had been, with lasting effects on Sean and now his brother. "Geoff, you can't avoid asking her out because some other girl was rude. Just because it didn't go well for Sean, doesn't mean it won't be great for you. Every relationship is different. You should follow your heart and give this person a chance."

His eyes lit up hopefully. "You think?"

"Absolutely," I said, excited for him, and nervous for me. I'd given him such optimistic advice when all my life I've favored the practical approach. What was happening to me?

He smacked his palm on the table and nodded. "All right. I'll do it."

"Good for you." My mouth curved upward even as I realized something had changed inside me.

We talked for a bit longer before I thanked him for the coffee and headed home. The entire drive, my words echoed through my mind. *"Every person is different. You should follow your heart and give this person a chance."*

Maybe I ought to take my own advice. Maybe things would be different for me than they had been for my mom.

As with every night since I'd met him, I went to sleep thinking of Henry. This time I didn't force my thoughts away. Instead, I let my dreams run wild. As I drifted off, a smile spread across my face as I pictured a white dress, two beautiful children, and a life filled with laughter.

CHAPTER FIVE

I ARRIVED at Rachel's twenty minutes before obedience class on Thursday, excited to take a chance on Henry and not so enthusiastic to break things off with Craig tonight. I mean, dumping someone ranks about as fun as getting dumped. It would've been easier to cancel with an email, but ending things via the internet seemed cold.

As I walked up the path toward Rachel's apartment, I found her slumped in the wicker chair on her tiny front porch. Chester was cuddled in her lap, sucking on the head of a stuffed bear like it was a pacifier.

My pace slowed as I approached. "What's going on?"

She set her beloved dog gently on the ground, then lifted her sunglasses to reveal red-rimmed eyes. "I'm done with men."

My eyes widened. "I thought you had another date with George's friend Dillon tonight."

"Ha!" She said it as a joke, then she started cackling as if the joke were on her. "You were so right about everything, Ellen. I should've listened to you."

Uh-oh. "What happened?"

"I took a chance. That's what happened." She threw her arms in the air to express just how stupid she'd been. "You said compatibility is the key. You warned me not to go out with someone just because he looks hot with his shirt off."

My eyes narrowed. "Did he do something to you?"

"You mean Mr. Octopus Hands? Yeah, he *tried*." She smiled, sweetly. "He came by after work, was all over me, then had the nerve to be annoyed when I slowed things down."

My eyes narrowed in disgust. "What a dirtbag."

She inhaled deeply. "After our night at The Oasis, it felt like we were connecting, you know? So, I let my guard down."

I nodded. It hadn't been an official date, but I'd felt that way yesterday with Henry as we'd talked before, during, and after class. I'd told him personal details that I rarely shared with anyone and I sensed it had been the same way with him.

"Tonight, Dillon was a completely different person." Her face scrunched up. "Why didn't I listen to you? I should've had him fill out a dating application to see if he'd mark the box 'sleaze-ball temporarily disguised as a nice guy'."

"Oh, Rach." I pulled her stiff body into a hug. "You couldn't have known. Next time will be different."

She leaned against me, sniffled, then drew back.

"Exactly. Because there won't *be* a next time. If I ever get the absurd notion to date again, I will let you screen him thoroughly before I invest one ounce of feeling into him."

I reached out and squeezed her hand. "I'm so sorry, sweetie."

"Me, too." She checked her watch. "Do you want me to take Chester to class for you tonight so you can get ready for your second date with Craig? He sounds perfect for you, and I shouldn't have encouraged you to go after that other guy. Nothing came of that, did it?"

"No." Only that I'd let myself fall for him, pictured our life together, and felt blissfully happy all day long at the thought of seeing him tonight. But, Rachel's tear-streaked face proved what happened if you took a chance on a guy who wasn't compatible. Ouch. My heart sank as I decided not to risk it with Henry. "You sure you feel up for taking Chester?"

"Are you kidding? I'd love to." She grabbed his leash. "He's the only male worth spending time with anyway. Er, except for Craig. He sounds nice and not like he'd maul you on the second date. Plus, you know his history and what he wants for the future. He's not someone just looking to hook up."

"Right," I said.

Then, I went home to get ready for the date with the man who I knew wanted the same things I did. I told myself over and over that this was the right thing to do. Unfortunately, it didn't help the emptiness I felt inside, missing my last chance to spend time with Henry.

SINCE CRAIG WAS VENTURING OUT into the wild world of ethnic cuisine, I met him for dinner at an Indian restaurant in downtown Sac near the state capitol building. Thirty minutes into our conversation and his notepad made another appearance. Not just to check stuff off this time, either. We'd apparently graduated into actual note taking.

"What is your stance on public education?" Craig poised his pen above the small lined pages. "Do you plan to send your children to the local school or are you thinking a private education would be better?"

"I don't have any kids," I said, wishing I could eat my samosas without an inquisition.

"Of course you don't have children yet. I've read your Detailed Dating profile multiple times," he pointed out patiently. "I'm forecasting for the future. Trying to assess any potential conflicts we might have in child rearing."

I shrugged. "As long as it's a good school, I'd be fine with either."

"Very flexible." He sounded impressed as he scratched something off his list and then wrote a word with an exclamation point after it.

I reached for my water, drained my glass, and couldn't help feeling like I'd stood up Henry. Had he been disappointed that I'd skipped the last class? Had he been up all night again doing whatever caused those dark circles under his eyes? Had he asked Rachel about me? Had he asked Rachel out? The thought made me sick to my stomach.

"Ellen?"

Craig's confused tone brought me back to the table and the fact that I was on a date. "What did you say?"

His brows furrowed. "How much did you miss?"

"The whole thing," I admitted, wondering if Kenzie had mastered her "special project" today, whatever it was that Henry had chosen for that. I'd been hoping to cure Chester of his destructive issues, but, in actuality, I didn't think anything in the world—not even the peppy and perfect Abby Wilson—could rid the chew monster of that habit.

"Hello? Ellen?"

Oh, man. Had I missed what he'd asked for the second time? Focus, Ellen. "I'm so sorry, Hen—I mean, Craig. Would you mind repeating that?"

He took a deep breath, wrote something down (not flattering, I presumed) and then cleared his throat. "I asked what you would do if you've been married ten years and . . .?"

I waited, but he didn't finish. "And what?"

"Just making sure you were listening this time." He seemed relieved that I had been. "If you've been married ten years, your husband was in an automobile accident—through no fault of his own, mind you—and he became crippled."

A horrible image popped into my head of Henry riding his bike and getting hit by a speeding car. I flinched. "That's a terrible thought."

He lifted his fork, eyed his masala suspiciously, then set it back down again without taking a bite. "Unfortunately, we can't predict what life will throw at us, but I think it's helpful to know how you would handle something that tragic."

The thought of Henry losing the use of his legs made me ill. But he'd survived losing his parents, and I knew in my heart he could survive anything life might hand him. "When I get married, it will be for better or for worse. If there's a worse, I'll do everything in my power to help my partner."

"I completely agree." Craig smiled, then made a check mark in his notes. "What are your thoughts on—"

"I'm sorry, but this isn't working." I signaled the waiter for our check.

Holding the pen between his fingers, Craig scratched his temple. "Did my scenario upset you?"

"No. Yes . . ." I splayed my hands on the table and leaned forward. "This is only our second date and you're asking me how I'd handle a horrible accident if we were married when the truth is, we don't even know each other yet."

"What do you mean?" He unfolded what appeared to be my completed Detailed Dating questionnaire and gestured toward the pages in his notebook as if to prove the point. "I feel I know you quite well, and I'd be happy to answer any questions if you need more information about me. Complete and total honesty is important to making a relationship work."

"That's the thing, Craig. We've gathered a bunch of information about our likes and dislikes by exchanging emails for over a month, but that doesn't mean we know each other. Not really." I thought about Henry and how much I'd learned about him in our few exchanges. "You and I have no idea what jokes make the other person laugh. If there's *chemistry* and *vibe* when we touch. How important our families are to us. Or, what the other would do if we saw a dog stranded by the side of the highway, hungry and malnourished..."

"Let me reassure you on that last one." He nodded and clasped his hands together on the table. "I would call animal control or the SPCA immediately, give the location, and unless I was in a hurry, I'd wait near the dog until the proper authorities arrived."

My throat closed up. It's not that Craig wasn't nice, it's that the only thing that had ever intrigued me about him was our high Detailed Dating score. "You're a good guy, Craig." As the waiter was about to set the bill on the table, I handed him my credit card, and couldn't believe what I was about to say to my perfect match. "We're just not . . . compatible."

His eyes went wide and his mouth hung open a little. "We're not a hundred percent, sure, but we have potential that's worth exploring. Look here," he opened his note-book, pulled out our profiles and showed me a number at the top of the paper that read, *"98% match."* Then, he flipped to the last page of his notes where he'd drafted some kind of spreadsheet and pointed to the line at the bottom. "According to my own personal observations, it's 84% likely that you're the one for me."

The straight A student in me (yeah, yeah, A-/B+) immediately felt insulted, so I rotated the book toward me and scanned his notes. "Let me see that."

"The closest any other woman has come is 62%, and that was five months ago." He sounded as if I should be proud of that score.

With an 84%? Yeah, right.

Hmmm. I'd been marked down 4% for making fun of him with the restaurant food critic remark (his loss, that had been a good one), 2% for hesitating between answers, and 5% each time he'd had to repeat himself tonight when I hadn't been paying attention, which was valid but should've put me at the low A range, not mid B range. "When, I'd like to know, did I ever hesitate between answers?"

He pointed to the prior page. "First, at the beginning of our meal when I inquired if you cooked."

My mouth dropped open. "Well, I was trying to decide if microwaving counted."

His finger slid down the page to a sentence with an asterisk next to it. "Second, when I asked if you set the toilet paper roll facing up or down."

I squeezed the cloth napkin in my lap. "No fair, I'd been chewing my food."

"I'll accept that." He made some slashes and calculations, then adjusted my score to 86%. "See, we're even more compatible than I thought."

Um, somehow we'd gotten off the point. Oops. "You're going to make some woman very happy, Craig. You really are."

"I'm willing to improve on areas you feel need work, Ellen. It feels a little early in the relationship, but we can explore the *chemistry* and *vibe* thing if you'd like." He put his hand over mine and . . . nothing.

No zip. No spark. And no wonder . . . he wasn't Henry. I patted his hand, then signed the credit card slip the waiter had set down. "The truth is, Craig, on paper it does read like we're compatible. And I can't explain it, other than to say I know in my heart that we aren't."

He bowed his head a moment and then nodded. "I certainly appreciate your honesty. Thank you for getting the check."

"You're welcome," I said, as we both stood. "Best of luck to you."

"To you as well." He started to hand me the boxes of leftovers until I waved my hand indicating he could keep them. It was the least I could do. "I hope you find what you're looking for," he said.

I smiled and thanked him even though it'd be impossible to find what I'm looking for when I didn't know what that was anymore. I'd wanted someone compatible, and even with a 98% match (the lame 86% doesn't count) from Detailed Dating, all I could think about was Henry. Checking my watch, I saw that the final doggy class had ended—along with my last chance to see Henry.

I tossed and turned in bed that night, trying to push Henry out of my mind. My head battled with my heart for hours, but eventually my heart won out and I let the few memories we'd shared wash over me. Curled up in my comforter, I replayed our conversations in my head. Every elbow nudge. Every laugh. Every touch. I wished I'd asked outright what he'd been up to that was so "intense." I wished I'd let him know I was interested. And more than anything, I wished I could see those deep gray eyes again.

CHAPTER SIX

MY COFFEE INTAKE doubled Friday morning and I still barely had the energy to make it to work. Too much tossing and turning all night.

I parked my car and dragged my feet across the employee parking lot, debating swallowing my pride to ask Rach if Henry had said anything about my missing class. But then, what would be the point? He'd never shown anything other than friendly interest in me, so the logical thing to do was move on. Right? Ugh. Why did dating have to be so complicated?

To distract myself from my dating debacles, I focused on customer reports all morning, and was deep into typing up a customer inquiry for our sales team (it had been a pleasant call for a change) when my phone beeped.

I leaned toward the speaker. "Yes?"

"Hi, Ellen." Ginger's perky receptionist voice rang out. "Gilbert Watson would like to see you in the lobby."

Frowning, I remembered it was Friday and checked my watch. "Didn't he already meet with tech support?"

"Yes, but he specifically asked to speak with you now." Her voice lowered. "He's very insistent."

Why didn't that surprise me? "I'll be right out."

With a few keystrokes on the computer, I checked Gilbert Watson's file to see if tech support (aka: Teddy) had solved our client's laptop issues. No updates. Great, I had to walk out blind.

I straightened my blouse, headed toward the lobby, and prepared myself for another rant from Gilbert Watson on how our software program was to blame for his computer issues and that we needed to pay up.

Pasting a smile on my face, I approached the tall elderly man in the lobby who stood next to a woman with short, curly white hair. "Good morning, Mr. Watson. I'm Ellen, the customer service rep you spoke with on the phone. How was your meeting with tech support?"

He introduced me to his wife, then to my utter astonishment, pumped my hand enthusiastically. "Wouldn't you know, it turns out I downloaded myself a virus containing spyware that slowed my computer and even made it stop sometimes. Had nothing to do with the software program after all."

Gee, that's exactly what I'd tried to tell him. Repeatedly. "I'm relieved to hear it wasn't our program, Mr. Watson."

His brows came together suddenly as he felt the empty breast pocket on his collared shirt. "Left my glasses in the restroom." Then he turned around. "I'll be right back."

Mrs. Watson chuckled as she watched the receptionist buzz her husband back to find his glasses. "Thank you for being so patient with Gilbert this past week, dear. When he gets it in his head that he's being taken advantage of, there's no reasoning with him. And from what I've heard, you've handled him very professionally. Can't tell you how many times I've made him apologize over the years."

Her admission made my mouth curve upward, especially since he'd insisted several times that his wife agreed with him. "If you don't mind my asking, how long have you been married?"

Her forehead crinkled and she tapped each finger against her thumb, counting. "It'll be fifty-two years this October."

Clearly my lack of sleep had taken its toll on my professionalism because I blurted out, "What made you decide to marry him?"

Smiling, as if the answer was obvious, she said, "Gilbert? Well, I loved him, of course."

With five decades of marriage under her belt, this woman had to know the secret to making marriage work. "Yes, but how'd you know that you were compatible? You must've had the same life goals so you knew there wouldn't be conflicts, right?"

Did my tone sound as desperate as I felt?

"Throughout our marriage, I'm guessing our 'life goals,' as you put it, have changed at least half a dozen times. As far as conflicts go? That man can drive me crazy as no one else in the world can, I assure you." She slid the back of her hand across her forehead as if to wipe pretend sweat away. "Still, I couldn't imagine spending my life with anyone else but Gilbert."

She had to be kidding me. These were her magic words of wisdom? That she couldn't imagine living without him? "More than fifty percent of marriages end in divorce, Mrs. Watson. In order to make that lifelong decision, how did you know it would last forever?"

"I guess I didn't." She put her hand on my forearm. "But, I wasn't going to lose him because of statistics. I loved him and I went for it." She winked at me. "Good thing, too. Wouldn't you say?"

As if on cue, Gilbert strode into the lobby with his computer case slung over his shoulder and held up his glasses. "Forgot my laptop, too. Isn't that a hoot?"

"Gilbert." She nudged his arm. "What am I going to do with you?"

We said polite good-byes, and as I watched Mr. and Mrs. Watson head out of the lobby, holding hands after half a century of marriage, it felt like a blindfold had been lifted. There were no guarantees. If you love someone, you either go for it or you don't.

Wait. Love? Where had that come from? I hadn't even known Henry a week and I certainly didn't believe in love at first sight. What a ridiculous notion for a strong, smart woman. Storybook love doesn't exist in real life. Yet, when I'd first met Henry and looked into those deep, dark gray eyes... And every time I'd talked to him since...

It had *felt* like storybook love.

Okay, forget my pride. I had to find Rachel.

RACHEL CAME to the office after lunch and I stormed into her cubicle. "Where have you been?"

"Ran to the mall at lunch and guess what I got?" She smiled, apparently oblivious to my desperation, as she set a double handled silver shopping bag on her desk, pulled out a shiny white shoebox, and handed it to me. "Surprise!"

"No way." I lifted the top, pushed the tissue aside, and immediately recognized the stunning pair of red stilettos I'd tried on last week but passed on in favor of the more practical black boots. "You went back for these? What for?"

She pulled them out of the box and displayed them in the air as we both stared at them in awe. "After Chester made his little chew toy mistake, you wouldn't let me buy you new boots, so I decided to get you the pair you really wanted."

I slid my fingers over the smooth, sexy heels. "They're as gorgeous as I remember. Thanks." I gave her a quick hug. "You didn't have to do that."

"It's the least I could do after you introduced my sweet baby to Simply Skilled." She put the heels back in the box and leaned against her desk, wearing an excited expression. "Since yesterday was the last class, Abby Wilson let us choose a special skill for our babies to master and guess what? My smart boy can now do his business in a litter box!"

So much for breaking him of his destructive chew habit. "You trained your dog to use a litter box? Like a cat?"

"Yes." She nodded, enthusiastically. "In just one class, too. My baby is super smart."

Yeah, except when he's Hoovering globs of hair from my brush.

She let out a contented sigh. "Now, I don't have to go home at lunch to give him a potty break anymore. Isn't that cool?"

"As long as the other dogs don't make fun of him for it." At the joke, I immediately thought of Kenzie. "I'm glad you liked the Simply Skilled class."

Rach slid into her chair, spinning it to face me. "Loved it. Emily Post couldn't find a flaw with Abby Wilson's training."

"True," I said, though she wasn't the person from class I'd been thinking about. "So, did you meet Henry? Did he say anything about me?"

It felt like junior high but, when you're desperate, why mince words?

"Yes." Her forehead wrinkled as if she were rethinking the conversation. "He did ask about you, actually."

Each second that ticked by felt like torture. "And . . .?"

"Well, at first we introduced ourselves, he wondered where you were, yada yada." She waved her hand in the air as if to skip to the point. "Then, get this, he asked if I thought your dates with Craig were going anywhere."

My heart started pounding. That had to be a good sign. "Really?"

Her eyes narrowed. "Don't worry. I gave him a piece of my mind."

Oh, no. "W-what do you mean?"

She crossed her arms. "I told him plain and simple that if he liked you—and it kind of seemed like he did with the way he hung on every word I said—then he should've asked you out himself. Not go digging for information from your friend." She peeked up at me with a smug smile. "Then, he asked for your number."

The pounding in my chest upgraded to galloping. "He did?"

"Don't worry, I told him he was too late because you were out with that Detailed Dating guy again and how compatible you both were. Then, I *may* have gone off about why men pretend to be one way and then act another way . . . like Dillon pretending he was interested in me one minute and that I was just a hook-up the next. It's weak, you know?"

I didn't know whether to laugh or cry. It sounded as if Henry liked me, but Rach had told him off. "What did he say then? And why oh why didn't you give him my number?"

She gave me a confused look. "Um, because Craig seems way more compatible? Do I need to remind you of the Dillon fiasco?"

Her desk phone rang, but she let it go to voicemail so I went on, "Rach, I had it all wrong. You did the right thing with Dillon. You liked him and you went for it."

She leaned forward in her chair, then threw her hands up in a cheer. "And look how great that turned out."

"Here's the thing." I moved closer and lowered my voice so nobody else could hear because adjacent cubicles tended to have big ears and at this point the lunch hour was way over. "Fifty percent of marriages end in divorce. And like how many people do we date before we even get married? A lot. Right?"

Her face went slack. "F-Y-I, if this speech is supposed to be uplifting, you need to rewrite it."

"My point is that despite all my convictions about compatibility, I wasn't really looking for the love of my life. With all my calculations, I ruled guys out before I'd ever given them a chance. If I'm interested in someone, I can't cross him out because he prefers hang gliding over strolls on the beach. If I do, I could miss an amazing fifty-two year marriage that's still going strong."

She ignored the ringing phone on her desk and shook her head. "You lost me."

I covered my face with my hands. "I can't stop thinking about Henry."

"Henry?" She looked thoroughly confused. "What happened to Craig? I thought you had everything in common."

I threw my hands out. "We're compatible in many ways. He'd be a logical, safe choice, but . . . I'm not interested. Isn't that ironic?"

"Painfully so."

Tears filled my eyes. "I should've gone to Simply Skilled

yesterday. It's where I *wanted* to be. But it scared me how much I liked Henry so I went for my safety date. And the entire time, I kept wishing I'd been in class with Henry."

Her eyes widened as if she'd just thought of something, then she fished in her handbag and pulled out a white envelope. "This might not be a good time to do this, but Henry asked me to give this to you. He didn't say what it was."

Rachel's telephone went *beep* and Ginger announced that Rach had an important call waiting and that the customer had been unable to reach her. She gave me a regretful look and I shooed her to take it since, you know, we were at work and that's kind of what they paid us to do.

I went back to my cubicle, ripped open the envelope, and emptied the contents into the palm of my hand. A silver dog bone-shaped piece of metal shined up at me, attached to a key ring. The silver bone was embossed with cursive lettering that read *Ellen*, and when I flipped it over it said *Auntie of the Year*. Even as my eyes burned, I laughed, remembering how I kept telling Henry I hoped to win Auntie of the Year from all my dog duty with Chester.

I fingered the tiny gift in my hand, thinking I'd never received a more wonderful present and wanting, more than anything, to call and thank him for it. My throat tightened, knowing I'd blown something special. And Rach had ruined any chance for repair.

Maybe storybook romance did exist, but I was the bone-head princess kicking the prince to the curb before he'd had a chance to ask me to the ball. Or, even better, to a picnic by the dog park.

AFTER WORK, I sat on my couch debating whether or not searching "Henry Holbrook III" online would make me creepy-obsessive. As I weighed the pros and cons of internet stalking, my mom called on her way home to tell me where she'd made dinner reservations before we hit the art show tonight.

I'd tried to keep my voice upbeat to hide my miserable mood, but apparently I'd done a lousy job because as we were wrapping up, my mom said, "Is something wrong? You sound down. Are things not going well with your new man?"

"Who? Oh, Craig." I'd forgotten about him. I sat on my couch and hugged one of the embroidered pillows to my chest for comfort. "No, I broke that off."

"Why?" Mom's voice oozed with sympathy. "He sounded perfect."

No, apparently just eighty-six percent. "He kept a chart, Mom. To rate how compatible we are."

Long pause. "How'd you do?"

I bolted upright. "Mother!"

"What?" She used her innocent tone. "I want to know your score. Any man who didn't think you were a catch is doing the math wrong."

"You know, it doesn't even matter." I dropped back into

the cushions and took a big breath. "I'm interested in someone else."

Not that it mattered at this point.

"The other man from Detailed Dating?" I could hear the *humm* of her garage door going up and knew she'd arrived home.

"No." I bit my lip, hoping I'd have her support. "From, uh, doggy class. I took Rachel's miniature beagle when I was puppy sitting, long story, and that's where I met Henry. He adopted a stray dog and signed her up for obedience school. Isn't that sweet?"

Short pause, then I heard a car door slam. "But you don't like dogs."

Why did everyone keep saying that? "I do, too."

"I've known you since birth and you've never expressed a smidgeon of interest in animals." Then she laughed. "Remember when you were in high school and Frank brought home his sister's King Charles Spaniel, Bitsy? You ran around the house with that lint remover permanently attached to your hand until the day she picked her up."

I rolled my eyes at the mention of Mom's Hubby Number Two. "That was fifteen years ago."

Not that a lint remover wouldn't come in handy with a dog around...

"All right, honey. He has a dog and you love dogs." She snickered. "What else do you know about him?"

"He's sweet. Funny." I fingered the dog bone keychain in my hand. "Thoughtful."

"Hmmm."

My stomach clenched at her disapproving tone. "What?"

She sighed. "Sweet and funny seem nice in the beginning, but they won't keep the relationship going long-term. What are his goals? What are his interests? I thought we decided Detailed Dating was the way to go. Those men are looking for serious relationships and they lay it all on the line. That's how I met Robert. Online dating."

My jaw clenched. "You don't even know Henry. How can you just rule him out?"

"It sounds like you don't know him very well either." She cleared her throat. "I'm not trying to upset you, Ellen. I want you to be smart so you don't get hurt. Lasting relationships are about compatibility."

Tears burned my eyes. "How would you know?"

"After two failed marriages, I think—"

"Don't forget about my dad." Okay, my voice might've sounded a tad sharp.

"Well, I never married him so—"

"He doesn't count. I've heard it before. You know what? That's your life, not mine, and you don't have all the answers. Who even knows what will happen with your marriage to Robert? You haven't even had your first anniversary yet."

"Ellen!"

"You think you know what's best for me, but you don't." My throat felt raw as I gripped the phone against my ear. "I'm not interested in online dating anymore. The three pet classes with Henry felt like three of the best dates I've ever been on. It was different with him. Not a crush, or infatuation, it felt . . . right. It doesn't make sense, but I can't explain it any other way."

Silence.

"I've blown it with him anyway and you're probably glad. But, I can't date who *you* think is right for me. I'm thirty years old, Mom. I need to live my life my way." I swiped at my wet cheeks. "I have to go."

"I will see you tonight." Her voice was tight and firm.

Grunting in frustration, I turned my phone off and tossed it on the cushion next to me. Oh, man. I'd never talked to my mom like that before. Well, not since my teen years, anyway. Great. Dinner and the art show should be such a blast. Not.

As I rubbed my temples, the white box on my coffee table caught my eye and called to me. So, even though I felt miserable, I tried on my red stilettos. They fit perfectly, and I took them for a test loop around my living room. Amazing. Sleek red heels actually made walking more fun. I'd loved these shoes the moment I'd tried them on, but I'd gone for the safety pair instead. Smart and sensible. That's me.

Or, that *had* been me. I promised myself that from now on, I was going to start choosing the shoes I really wanted. Ditto on men.

CHAPTER SEVEN

AFTER THE HORRIBLE phone conversation with my mom, I took a long hot bath, hoping to soak away my troubles. No such luck. Now, wearing nothing but a bathrobe, I opened my front door and stared miserably at Rachel, who looked gorgeous in a jade green dress. "Forget tonight. I'm not going."

"Turn." She made a circular motion with her finger, shut the door behind her, then nudged me toward my bedroom. "Change."

With Rachel's hand planted firmly on my back, I dragged my feet as I moved forward begrudgingly. "I had an awful fight with my mom."

"Really?" She headed straight for my closet, flipped through my clothes, and eyed a beige dress up and down before dismissing it. "What about?"

I dropped back on my bed. "Thirty years of pent up

aggression, I think. She's hounding me to get back to Detailed Dating. I told her I'm only interested in one person, and she was less than thrilled with my choice." I sat up suddenly. "Do you think tracking down Henry on the internet would be going overboard?"

"No need." She selected a sexy black and red silk camisole from my closet and handed it to me. "I took care of it."

Every muscle in my body froze. "Y-you what?"

She gave an exaggerated shrug. "I called All Things Furry, spoke to Abby Wilson, and used my powers of persuasion to get Henry's phone number. Then I called him, admitted I'd jumped to conclusions about your liking that Detailed Dating guy, and told him which art gallery we'd be at tonight if he wanted to meet up with us."

I squealed. "You did? Seriously?"

"Yes, which is why you need to get dressed." She grabbed my hand and pulled me to my feet. "He kinda came across stunned when I mentioned we were going to the art showing, so I told him we were quite cultural, thank you very much."

I threw my arms around her. "I love you, Rach. You've taken the term 'best friend' to a whole new level."

"Oof." She patted me on the back as I tightened my grip. "It was the least I could do after my negative vibes from my Dillon drama botched your cute flirtation. I can't believe I lost two days of my life being depressed over that twig."

"He was so not worth it." I slipped out of my bathrobe,

then into a black skirt and the dressy tank Rach picked out. "How did Henry sound when you called?"

"Surprised." She held her hands up. "But in a good way."

"And he said he'd meet us?"

She tapped a crimson painted fingernail against her chin. "Not specifically, but he seemed interested."

My stomach clenched. "What if he doesn't come?"

"That wouldn't be a good sign." Apparently noticing the disappointed look I felt spread across my face, she waved a hand dismissively. "I'm sure he will, though."

Checking my watch, I saw we were running late to meet my mom and Robert for dinner. I zipped to the bathroom, did a re-touch on my make-up, ran a brush through my hair, then checked myself in the mirror. My cheeks were flushed, my eyes wide, and I tucked my shoulder-length hair behind my ears. This silky tank and black skirt was a lot sexier than anything Henry had seen me wear to doggy class. Not exactly attire for practical black boots. This ensemble screamed red high heels all the way.

I hurried to the living room and slipped into my gorgeous red stilettos. Every nerve in my body felt anxious. What if he didn't show?

I couldn't think like that.

Because what if he *did* show.

Taking a deep breath, I opened the front door, and held my head high. "I'm ready."

No more playing it safe.

If Henry came to the art gallery tonight, I'd reveal my feelings to him.

As we walked into Ripple Art Gallery in downtown Sacramento, my mom and I sped off in different directions.

"Gee, that dinner wasn't uncomfortable or anything." Rachel accepted a glass of champagne from a server, handed me a flute, and steered me toward an abstract painting that would've looked great in my living room.

"How does *she* have the nerve to be mad at *me*?" I pointed to my chest. "That's what I'd like to know."

Rach raised a sarcastic brow. "Perhaps because you insulted her marriage? Insinuated it wouldn't last?"

Oh, right. That. "I was trying to illustrate that she didn't have all the answers."

"Nice approach." She clinked her glass to mine. "Not."

I sipped my champagne, then surveyed the large, trendy room that was divided by tall, detached, white walls that stood solidly beneath the high black pipe-exposed ceiling. The place was packed. Seemed like all of Sacramento had turned up for this art gallery's opening. Everyone except one person. I turned back to the painting, trying not to show my disappointment. "I don't see him."

"Relax. We just got here." She pivoted slowly, her eyes scanning the room. "Wait . . . yes, I think that's him behind that wooden beam. Nice and early, too. Not exactly playing hard to get."

I gasped. "Where?"

"Back left corner of the room." She squinted, then put a hand to her mouth. "Oh, wow."

"What?" I demanded, not daring to turn around.

"Yesterday he'd been wearing sweats and had major stubble."

Sounded familiar to me. "And?"

Her eyes descended presumably from his head down to his toes. "Let's just say, he sure cleans up well."

As my heart thumped in my chest, I peeked over my shoulder. My eyes skipped past groups of people chatting, sipping champagne, and tasting hors d'oeuvres, until they came to rest on a *GQ* version of Henry. *Wow* was an understatement. He'd transitioned from sexy in an understated way to absolutely gorgeous in a universal cover model way. He wore slacks, a black collared shirt, and his tousled hair complimented his now clean-shaven face. Even from across the room, his eyes still got me, too. Deep, dark, and mysterious as he listened to whatever a woman with golden locks cascading over her shoulder was saying to him.

I grabbed Rachel's forearm. "Who's he talking to?"

"Ouch." She yanked her arm away. "Get a grip, girl."

Turning on my heel, I pretended to study a black and white painting. "If he's trying to make me jealous, it's working."

Buzzing chatter filled the room and a couple pushed their way toward the painting we were pretty much blocking, so we scooted down the wall to the next one. "Think about it, Ellen. Why would he come meet you at this art gallery if he was on a date? That makes no sense."

I nodded, thankful for her logic. "Good point."

Then we both watched as the beautiful woman put an arm around Henry, gestured to the painting next to them, then whispered something close to his ear.

A pang jolted through me. "She must be a really good friend."

"Well, you'll never know who she is until you ask." She laced her arm through mine and led me in his direction. "You were all desperate that you'd never see him again and now he's here. So, go get him."

The shy part of me wanted to run the other way, but I forced myself to keep walking. What if Rach had it wrong? What if he really was out on a date and had only come to meet us to be polite? Just a night out to talk about the dogs and what they'd learned in class?

"Good luck," Rachel whispered, then made herself scarce.

When I was still several feet away, he glanced up, and met my gaze. As I approached slowly—turns out sexy heels are no picnic to balance in—I swear he did a double-take. Excitement flitted through me. He wasn't the only one who'd gone from casual to sexy.

"Excuse me," he said to the woman, then came toward me until we were standing face to face. "Ellen."

"Henry." Here he was, right in front of me, the guy I'd been obsessing over. And I could see why. Whether in sweats or slacks, he made me all gooey inside. He stood mere inches away and I could barely resist doing what every part of me wanted to do—snuggle up to him and breathe in his delicious musky cologne without space between us. "Thank you for the keychain," I said, finally.

He looked almost shy for a moment. "I thought I'd be giving it to you in person. I was surprised when you skipped the last class. Your friend Rachel said you were . . . busy."

So much for small talk. "Oh, that. Yeah, I'd been trying to fulfill a dating theory."

He gave me a curious look, like he wasn't sure if I was kidding or not. "You mean an experiment?"

"Exactly." Without thinking, I tapped the back of my hand against his chest, which was solid in a very distracting way. Where was I? Oh, right. Baring my soul. Breathe, Ellen. "I've had this idea about love. That in order to find it and for it to last, I had to make sure to meet someone who had the same goals and interests as me, which is why I signed up for Detailed Dating. You remember, that online dating website—"

"—with the red pen." He raised his brows in a playful way. "Right."

"Good memory." I lifted my glass toward him, trying to lighten the mood. "Through their recommended matches, I screened profiles, ruled out a few with probable conflicts, then emailed ten potentials. Out of those, only two made it past my third week of email screening."

When I paused for a moment, he said, "And?"

I bit my lip, remembering back. "My first date was scheduled the same night I met you."

He ran a hand through his hair, making it look even sexier. "You mentioned the next day you were seeing someone you met online, but your friend said that's over?"

I nodded.

"What happened?"

I took a bracing breath. "Last night, I almost called my date 'Henry.'" My face flushed. "What does that tell you?"

The sides of his mouth turned upward. "I'd rather hear from you what it means."

Mustering all of my courage, I blurted, "Dog class with you felt like a better date than the ones with my supposedly perfect match."

"Really?" His smile grew and, if I wasn't mistaken, he looked relieved. "Then why would you miss our last class?"

Our? As in Kenzie and him? Or him and me? So many ways to read one little word and I felt like asking him to clarify. Instead, I went with, "Last minute change of plans. Actually, I stopped by Rachel's to pick up Chester when—"

"Sorry to interrupt." The woman in the sleek black business suit with the world's worst timing, suddenly appeared beside Henry. She gave me an odd look, then put a possessive arm around him. "Mind if I have a word with the artist? Important business to discuss."

"Artist?" Confused, my gaze passed back and forth between them.

"Why, yes." The woman, who stood several inches taller

than me, handed me a glossy brochure. "Aren't you here to see Henry's work?"

With my left hand still holding my champagne glass, I read the brochure in my right hand, which featured paintings by Henry Holbrook III. My jaw went slack. So that's how he could spend every day in sweats. He'd been creating those beautiful paintings I'd admired. No wonder they'd moved me. Just like he always did. "You're the artist being showcased tonight?"

Henry nodded, his eyes studying mine. He looked like he wanted to tell me something, but held back. I also noticed he didn't ask the lady to remove the arm she'd placed around his waist.

"Didn't you know?" the woman raised a perfectly penciled brow.

"No." My blood ran cold as I realized what this meant. He was here for work and not to see me. No wonder Henry had sounded surprised when Rachel told him we were coming here. My heart sank.

"I'm Jennifer Cooke, owner of Ripple Art Gallery." She reached out to shake my hand. "Thank you so much for coming tonight. If you'll excuse us for a moment, I need to discuss something in private with Henry."

"Of course." Never mind that she hadn't bothered to ask my name because she obviously didn't care. I quickly stepped away, feeling totally humiliated. I'd thought he'd come here for me. The fact that Rach and I were at his art showing tonight was just dumb luck.

And I'd poured my heart out to him. This is exactly what I got for not playing it safe.

I circled the room and sipped my champagne as if I weren't totally falling apart on the inside. Where was Rachel when I needed her? Had I totally imagined that Henry had seemed relieved by what I'd told him? Did he like me or not? Because one thing was perfectly obvious, the owner of the art gallery wanted more out of Henry Holbrook III than a commission on his paintings.

As if my nerves weren't raw enough from my encounter with the art gallery owner and Henry, my mother picked this exact moment to approach me. "Young lady, who were you talking to?"

Really? She had to do this to me now? "Um, have you seen Rach? I need her."

"Was he the crush you were telling me about on the phone earlier?" she said, hot on my heels as I tried desperately to find my friend.

"Keep your voice down." I gave her my scary look. "And it's not a crush."

More like a crush on steroids.

"That was Henry, right?"

I stopped in my tracks. "How do you know his name?"

She held up the brochure, complete with a photo of the artist, as tears filled her eyes. "I'm sorry I gave you a hard time earlier. You're my little girl and I didn't want you to get hurt. But, I think you should trust your instincts on this one."

My jaw dropped. "Who are you and what have you done with my mom?"

She gave a short laugh, then wiped a tear that slipped down her cheek. "I've made my share of mistakes with men. Believe me, I don't think I have all the answers." Her voice filled with emotion. "I was just trying to look out for you."

"I know, Mom." Overwhelmed by her sudden (and strange) change of heart, I put my arm around her and gave her a side hug. "I'm sorry for what I said on the phone about you and Robert. You both seem really happy together."

She kissed me on the cheek. "It's about time for me, isn't it? I'm sure it'll be that way for you, too."

I spotted Henry and Jennifer across the room. "Definitely not any time soon."

Not with Jennifer Cooke around. She was clearly the better match for him. In addition to being confident and beautiful, she and Henry shared passion for the art world. I, on the other hand, had taken art history pass/fail so it wouldn't ruin my GPA.

"Oh, Ellen." My mom squeezed me around the waist. "He's not interested in her."

"Are you not seeing what I'm seeing? That's the owner of the art gallery, Mom." I gestured toward where they were having a serious discussion. Jennifer had her arm around him, yet again. "Face it, she's way better suited for him. I can't even tell a Monet from a Sisley. Well, not unless there's a water lily involved."

"Oh, I'm sure that's just business," she said, dismissively.

This was getting scary. My very practical mom had sudden faith in Henry? An artist? Not exactly the stable career choice she'd normally opt for. Although a lot of his paintings did have a SOLD card placed over the title. I was about to ask Mom about her new attitude when Jennifer detached herself from Henry and strode off toward the front of the room. At the same time, my mom told me she needed to go check on something.

Out of nowhere, a face appeared in front of me. "Ellen."

I jumped back. "Rachel! Where have you been?"

"Major emergency." She held up her cell phone. "Gina finally broke up with George. She needs me to come over pronto. I want to bring champagne and celebrate, but obviously she's not there yet."

"No, I'd wait on that one." I sighed. "Guess my mom can take me home. Another love bites the dust."

"Yeah, but we knew their days were numbered." She gave me a concerned look. "Oh, wait. Did you mean Gina or you? What's wrong? Why aren't you with Henry?"

"The owner of the art gallery, that's why." A waiter strode by and swapped my empty champagne glass for a new one. "Henry's the artist she's showcasing tonight and judging by her actions, she'd like to showcase more than his paintings."

Rach threw her head back and laughed. "That's a good one."

Not the sympathetic response I'd expected. "Are you laughing at my misery?"

"Oh, please." She fiddled in her purse for her keys, then adjusted the strap on her shoulder. "First, you thought he was after Abby-what's-her-name. Now, he's after the art gallery owner? Stake your claim and get on with it."

I pointed across the room. "You saw her hanging on him."

"Yeah, I saw *her* when I should be seeing *you*." She glanced behind me. "He's directly across the room, talking to some guy, so stop making excuses and go for it."

My pulse rate picked up. "How?"

"Show me less jealousy and more action." Her voice held an edge of 'duh' to it. "I'll tell Gina you're thinking of her. Bye."

My eyes narrowed at her as she slinked out the door. Mostly because she was right. I knew it was time to face my fears. I downed my champagne, set the empty glass on a table, and headed toward Henry.

MY HEELS CLICKED across the gallery's hardwood floor and my heart pounded in my ears. I'd confront Henry, once and for all, and nothing would stop me this time.

"Ellen!" a female voice cheered.

I flipped my head around to see our perky blonde dog obedience instructor. "Abby?"

She bounced over and threw her arms around me. "We missed you yesterday, but Rachel's such a sweetie, too."

I peered around Abby, but couldn't see where Henry had gone. "I heard Chester learned a special talent."

"It was fabulous. That cute snickerdoodle will do anything for a treat. And you probably already know that Kenzie learned how to shake. Sweet angel put her paw right in my hand. Exciting progress, huh?"

"Yes." My heart warmed that Kenzie was learning to trust people. But why would Abby assume I knew about Henry's dog?

"Come." She led me over to a group of people I recognized from the Simply Skilled class: the elderly woman who owned the poodle, the mom with the outspoken boy, the young guy with the bulldog, and a few more. "Look who I found, everyone."

We exchanged cheerful greetings and it made me nostalgic for doggy class, Kenzie, and even crazy Chester. Abby latched onto the arm of a very handsome man who smiled down at her. Okay, maybe I'd jumped to conclusions when it came to Abby. But, I still didn't feel secure about Jennifer Cooke.

Abby's eyes shot just above my shoulder and she waved. "Henry! Thanks so much for inviting us to see your amazing work. Especially the—"

"Thank you all for coming," he said.

His shoulder brushed mine as he came up next to me.

Everyone started giving us looks, and I wondered if they knew something I didn't. Maybe I could get them to signal with a thumbs up or down?

Henry's hand wrapped gently around my elbow. "Would you excuse us?" he said to the others.

They murmured affirmative remarks and before I knew it, Henry and I were walking away from the group and toward the left side of the gallery, which seemed to be a quieter area.

Finally, he stopped and faced me with an apologetic look. "Sorry about the interruption earlier. Jennifer had a business question she needed to ask me."

Time to jump. "Why didn't you ever tell me you're an artist?"

His facial expression changed. "Well, because it's only recently that I've actually made a living at it."

My mouth twisted. "Why would that matter?"

He hesitated a moment. "When I found that pen, you told me you were really into Detailed Dating . . ."

Was I mistaken or did he look nervous? "So?"

His gray eyes flooded with emotion. "I looked up your profile online."

Oh, man. I'd laid out in detail exactly what would and wouldn't work for me in a relationship. No exceptions allowed and an artist probably wouldn't have made the cut. "You, uh, did?"

"Hard as that is to admit, yes." His gaze stayed on mine. "Everything in your profile told me you're organized, know what you want, and, to be honest, it seemed like an artist would rank low on your professional stability requirement."

Oh, man. Why did I have to be so anal? "But that was before I met you."

His shoulders relaxed. "So you might be willing to take a chance on an artist who has never tried online dating, never filled out a compatibility profile, and is hoping he never will?"

I wouldn't know the answer to his question until he revealed the mystery behind the dark circles under his eyes all week. "Is this why you were so tired in class? Because you were preparing for this show?"

He paused way too long. "Yes. I'd spent all night painting and well . . . it was important to me. That particular painting, I mean."

What was he holding back? "Are you and the owner of the art gallery . . . dating?"

His gray eyes widened. "You mean Jennifer and me?

"Yes." My cheeks heated as I braced myself for his answer.

"No." He shook his head and his forehead wrinkled. "Why would you think that?"

Oh, this was awkward. "She seems really into you."

"Well, I don't know about that, but there is no way she thinks *I'm* interested in *her*."

Now we were getting down to business. "Why not?"

He waited, his gaze intent on mine. "She just wouldn't think that. Trust me."

"How come you avoid answering my questions? Like

when you showed up to All Things Furry looking exhausted and mentioned you'd been talking to Abby Wilson after class. When I asked what you'd been doing the night before, I couldn't get a straight answer out of you. So, I assumed . . ."

His brows came together as he put two and two together, then his eyes bulged. "You thought Abby and I . . .?"

I pictured Abby and her hot date. Yeah, I'd been off the mark on that one. Still. . . "Well, how should I know? You were obviously hiding something."

His face sobered. "I was. But not what you think."

Wow. I couldn't believe he'd finally admitted it! "Well? Aren't you going to tell me what you'd really been doing?"

"No." His face turned serious. "I'm going to show you."

He slipped his hand in mine, causing tingles to wander up my arm as he led me to the opposite corner of the room. We squeezed by various people—some who were talking and others who were gazing appreciatively at the art around them—and I couldn't stop wondering what he'd been doing to cause those deep circles under his eyes.

In the very back of the room, we stopped in front of a painting . . . of me! It was entitled "Love at First Glance" and my breath caught. He'd captured my expression perfectly— it was the same first look I'd gone over a million times in my own mind, only from his viewpoint.

The painting focused on the woman's green eyes with brown flecks, *my* eyes, and the appreciative look I'd given Henry when he'd offered to rescue my friend's dog.

Tears blurred my vision as I stared at the painting. All this time I'd wondered what had caused those dark circles under his eyes. It had been the hours he'd spent picturing me in his mind, *painting* me. And all that time, I'd been thinking of him, too.

"Well?" He nudged my shoulder a little while still holding my hand. "Aren't you going to say something?"

My mouth opened, then quickly closed. What was that yellow card above the title? My head whipped around and I frowned up at him, accusingly. "The card above the title says *SOLD*."

He reached out to smooth my hair back from my face. "That's what Jennifer had to talk to me about earlier. It wasn't for sale and a woman insisted that she be allowed to buy it. Since she is someone I want to win over, I couldn't say no."

My mouth dropped open. First Abby, then Jennifer, and now another mystery woman? "Who would you sell my painting to in order to win her over?" But inside, I already knew.

He looked as if he were trying to hold in a laugh. "Your mother."

My lips twitched at the confirmation I'd been right. Even though we had our issues, I sure did love my mom. "She can be a little overbearing at times."

"Good to know." He tucked my hair behind my ear, brushed his lips past my cheek, then whispered. "She promised to let us come over any time to visit it."

Ha! So that's why my mom had been so sure about

Henry. She'd seen the painting. Anyone who saw it would know how much time, love and care had gone into each brush stroke. Even Jennifer Cooke. No wonder she'd given me a weird look when we met. She'd recognized me.

I tore my eyes from the painting, gazed up at Henry, and melted against him. "Henry?"

He played with my hair as his deep gray eyes met mine. "Yes?"

"You do realize you're going to have to ask me out, right?" I moistened my lips. "How can it be love at first glance when we've only attended doggy class together?"

He leaned his forehead against mine. "Every time I'm with you feels like a date."

I leaned close to his ear. "If that's the case, this makes number four."

His face took on a serious quality. "I'm going to ask you to marry me. Very soon."

My heart pounded in my chest. "I'm going to say yes."

His mouth crept into a small smile. "For now, I'm going to kiss you."

"It's about time." His lips pressed against my cheek again, heat igniting against my skin, and my shoulder curled in as I savored the feeling. "I was afraid I'd have to attend more doggy school before you ever made your move."

Finally, our mouths came together, and a blissful feeling settled over me. After all the hard work I'd gone through trying to find love, it had found me instead. Right as we started our second kiss, clapping erupted around us. We pulled back slowly and turned around to face a crowd.

Abby Wilson, standing front and center, whistled with two fingers in her mouth. The elderly woman winked knowingly at me. My mom stood next to Robert, teary-eyed and with a hand over her heart. Although I'd thought I should go with the safe and screened choices, my heart had told me to give this guy a chance. And I'm glad I did.

When it comes to men, there are no hard and fast rules. Sometimes online dating works out, sometimes it doesn't. You can use your head, follow your heart, or, with one single glance, you might just fall for that person who truly gets you and find your happiest place.

The End

Have you fallen in love with these characters, too? Find out what happens next with Gina's story:

The Pretend Promise
River City Sweethearts, Book 2

💙 **Join Susan's inner circle** for sneak peeks, swoon-worthy updates, and first dibs on her fresh, flirty & fabulous new releases—**subscribe now at** susanhatler.com/newsletter

ABOUT THE AUTHOR

SUSAN HATLER is a New York Times bestselling author of sweet, heartfelt romances filled with humor and emotion, as well as captivating young adult novels. Her books have charmed readers worldwide and have been translated from English into German, Italian, French, Spanish, Dutch, and Portuguese. A born optimist, Susan believes life is amazing, people are fascinating, and imagination is endless. She loves spending time with her unforgettable characters—and hopes you will, too.

💜 **Join Susan's inner circle** for sneak peeks, swoon-worthy updates, and first dibs on her fresh, flirty & fabulous new releases—**subscribe now at** susanhatler.com/newsletter

Stay connected with Susan:
Website: susanhatler.com

TITLES BY SUSAN HATLER

River City Sweethearts Series
The Happiest Place
The Pretend Promise
The Accidental Valentine
The Safest Harbor
The Mischievous Matchmaker
The Healing House
The Promotion Proposal
The Brightest Tomorrow
The Beloved Bakery
The Sweetest Mistake

Blue Moon Bay Series
The Second Chance Inn
The Sisterhood Promise
The Wishing Star
The Friendly Cottage
The Christmas Cabin
The Oopsie Island
The Wedding Boutique
The Holiday Shoppe

TITLES BY SUSAN HATLER

Do-Over Date Series
Million Dollar Date
The Double Date Disaster
The Date Next Door
Date to the Rescue
The Dashing Date
Once Upon a Date
The Island Date
One Fine Date
The Date Mistake
The Decadent Date

The Wedding Whisperer Series
The Wedding Charm
The Wedding Connection
My Wedding Date
The Wedding Bet
The Wedding Promise

TITLES BY SUSAN HATLER

Christmas Mountain Romance Series

The Christmas Compromise

'Twas the Kiss Before Christmas

A Sugar Plum Christmas

Fake Husband for Christmas

The Christmas Competition

A Gingerbread Christmas

A Silver Bells Christmas

Christmas with the Nanny Next Door

The Christmas PenPal

Creating Christmas Series

A Christmas to Belong

A Christmas to Shine

TITLES BY SUSAN HATLER

www.ingramcontent.com/pod-product-compliance
Lightning Source LLC
Chambersburg PA
CBHW020647170526
45242CB00029B/168